SARAH MORRELL

Hashtag PRESS

Published in Great Britain by Hashtag Press 2022



A CIP catalogue for this book is available from the British Library.

ISBN 978-1-9138351-5-6

Typeset in Garamond Classic 11.75/14.5 by Blaze Typesetting
Printed in Great Britain by Clays Ltd, St Ives plc

Hashtag PRESS

HASHTAG PRESS BOOKS
Hashtag Press Ltd
Kent, England, United Kingdom
Email: info@hashtagpress.co.uk
Website: www.hashtagpress.co.uk
Twitter: @hashtag_press

# ACKNOWLEDGEMENTS

A few special thank yous to a few special people who have supported me on my writing journey so far.

Firstly, to Helen and Abiola at Hashtag Press who saw through the tower of boxes two days before moving day and believed in my book pitch more than I could ever have hoped for.

To Mo and Pops for always encouraging my crazy ideas and projects and never once questioning that they may not occur, however spurious or far-fetched!

To my fabulous friends who have given their ears, often wiped away tears and shared more laughs and cake than is humanly possible.

To the most amazing husband in the world (yes, I realise I've written this down!) who is there for me always and especially in times of dry toast and Diet Coke.

And lastly to my three incredible kids who can achieve anything they put their minds to and inspire me beyond words every single day.

*For Claire. Forever missed x*

# CHAPTER ONE

## *Green Slippers*

I'm not a nasty person. Don't get me wrong, sometimes I can be a bit harsh towards Mum's cooking, but that's not being nasty—that's being truthful. Her cooking really is *dreadful.* I thought her curried coconut concoction was the worst until she made a saltfish stew last week, and believe me, it was the absolute pits!

There's only one thing I dislike more than Mum's cooking and that's birds. Sometimes I'm tempted to toss a dollop of Mum's menu mishaps to the annoying, feathered wing-rats constantly flapping outside my window, but even I wouldn't be so cruel. And that's after I got bird-mobbed last week and one pecked my ear and made it bleed. So, you see, I'm not a nasty person.

In fact, the only time I've ever liked Mum's cooking was when my best friends, Ruby and Anais, used to come around for tea—it was one of the few times Mum hung up her spatulas and ordered us pizza instead. Only they've not visited me for ages. We don't eat together at school anymore either. New girl Celeste Morton has made sure of that.

She thinks I'm boring because I like books and chess, which is really unfair because now Ruby and Anais have sided with her. I always thought the three of us had fun playing games and telling each other silly stories about our books, but lately, every time I've approached them to play, they've nudged each other and quickly scuttled away.

I even heard Celeste call me Fleur Marie 'Borer Snorer' behind my back the other day, and both Ruby and Anais giggled and made snoring sounds. I wanted to run home there and then, but I knew Nan would quiz me, so I ran into the toilets instead. Not that any of them bothered to check on me, which is why I'm pretty sure they won't want to play chess or draw like we used to. Not with Celeste firmly on the scene.

That's why I've been eating in the hall on my own and staying inside for breaks. Leena and Beau asked me to play with them but I'm not as into sports as they are. I've found something else to keep me occupied though: I clean the books and chess pieces in the library for Mr Augustus, which makes the time pass faster.

I only wish I wasn't doing it alone. I'd give anything to have some company and laugh over silly stories or illegal chess moves again, but that's not likely to happen anytime soon.

The cleaning task mainly involves wiping book covers with one of Mr Augustus's fusty, old cloths, and the occasional rubbing out of a rude word. I only knew a handful of rude words in the beginning, but by the end of term, I was pretty sure I could write a whole different type of alphabet. So, I did. Although Mum didn't seem too impressed when I updated her on 'Rude Alpha' progress during teatime that night.

"What do you mean you've been helping with the cleaning again?" Mum asked as she hovered the pepper pot above her crisp, not-officially-burnt chicken. "It's been a lovely sunny day today. Didn't you fancy going outside and playing with your friends?"

The truth is, I would love to hang out with Ruby and Anais again, but they're more interested in Celeste's fancy, new nail polish or incredible, new phone. Given I still bite my nails and can't afford a phone, I'd say I'm officially out of their cool club.

"No, not today," I lied. "Ruby's. . . err. . . still off with a sore throat and. . . Anais booked herself into. . ."

My nostrils flared in panic until I spotted Dad's guitar slumped next to the bookcase. It was exactly where he'd propped it up before he left us last year. "Booked herself into guitar practice!"

Phew. That was close. Mum was too busy dipping her chicken into her sauce to notice any hesitation, although it looked more like she was hammering a nail through her plate as her wavy, blonde hair bounced against her chin with every bash.

I didn't want to go into detail about why I'd suddenly been dropped by Ruby and Anais with anyone, let alone Mum. She would only worry, and she'd had more than enough to worry about recently. Plus, I didn't want her to feel bad that I was one of the last ten-year-olds in my class who still didn't have a phone. It would tip her towards working evenings and that was the only time Nan and I properly saw her.

"What about the new girl, Collette?" Mum asked, her beady, blue eyes flickering towards my coffee-coloured gaze.

"Can't you play with her? I'm sure she'd be glad of a new friend or two."

That was the problem, she had already found a new friend or two–*my* friends! And judging by the way Celeste always glared at me, she didn't seem keen on making it three.

"It's Celeste, not Collette, and we haven't really had a chance to chat much yet," I said.

Maybe it was the zing of the pepper sauce, but my eyes began to sting, and my cheeks suddenly felt hot. Mum had swallowed my fibs about Ruby, Anais, and Celeste, but she wasn't having the same success with her own crispy cooking. Every mouthful she took looked pained, and every chew of her dry chicken sounded like she was crunching glass.

"I picked you up a copy of *The Evening Gazette* tonight, Nell!" Mum shouted to Nan.

Nan was sitting at the opposite end of the table trying to hack a piece of meat from the bone using her fork rather than risking her dentures.

Nan isn't the slightest bit deaf, but ever since she started having dizzy spells after Grandpa Willie died and Dad left last summer, Mum has treated her like an old lady. Holding her by the elbow, buying straws for her drinks, talking to her more loudly, that kind of thing.

"Strange goings-on in Farrow Park again if the headline is anything to go by," Mum continued. "Another sighting of a flying hand! Can you imagine seeing that? A human hand, suspended mid-air, and spotted right above the hairdressers down the road. DOWN THE ROAD, NELL! And in broad daylight too. That's only next door but four hundred and thirty-seven from here. It doesn't make you feel safe in your own home, does it?" She looked up at Nan who didn't respond. "I SAID, IT DOESN'T MAKE YOU FEEL SAFE IN YOUR OWN HOME, DOES IT, NELL?"

I glanced over at Nan who was paying little attention to Mum's patronising patter, preferring instead to eye up the newspaper that she was holding below her pointy nose. Nan's clammy, dark skin shimmered underneath the light, which confirmed that the cutting up of Mum's chicken had definitely been a gruelling workout.

"According to this," Mum droned on, "police say they've found another slipper too. A green one this time, right at the top of a thirty-five-foot tree! I'm sure they said the last slipper they found was purple, and they retrieved that from the top of the Royal Meadow Infirmary's roof, do you remember?" She didn't wait for either of us to reply. "That building's got at least fifteen floors, so goodness knows how someone managed to get it all the way up there."

"What's a green slipper got to do with a flying hand?" I asked, as I nipped my nose to stop me from sneezing.

"I've no idea but I hope they've got plenty of police officers patrolling the streets. I mean, it's not right, is it? All these arms and legs and slippers flying about the place. Whatever next? Flying pigs?" Mum thumped the newspaper down on the empty chair next to Nan, and finally focused on her tea.

"Just the journalists' way of selling newspapers," Nan said. "Nothing to worry about." Thankfully Mum had her mouth full and couldn't answer. "Now, enough of all this slipper nonsense. Tell me, how did my favourite gran-baby get on at school today?"

Thank goodness for Nan! I love how she always asked me that question at teatime to give me a break from eating Mum's monstrous meals.

"Well, I found three new rude words today so only one more to go before 'Rude Alpha' completion! Do you want to hear the latest version?"

Nan nodded cheekily. She busily chomped on her sweet potato, which she would soon find out tasted nothing like her childhood dishes in St. Lucia, but rather bonfires instead.

"Hang on a minute," Mum interrupted. "I don't like the sound of this. Let's test one first."

"My pleasure." I grinned as I twirled one of my plaits. "Which letter would you like to hear?"

"Let's go for O," Nan mused, still bravely chewing on her ash-flavoured spud.

I knew Nan would back me up. She treats me like a proper person. Even though she always calls me her gran-baby, she never treats me like an actual baby–unlike Mum. I am almost eleven, after all.

I dived into my pocket to retrieve the handwritten list. "O. . . O." I ran my finger down the crumpled piece of paper until I reached the letter. "Here it is! O is for Old Hag," I said with a giggle.

Even Mum cracked a smile.

"There's nothing wrong with an old hag!" Nan said. She stroked her grey afro with the palm of her hand until it touched the tightly pinned bun at the back of her head. "No family is complete without one!" Her stony face finally softened with a sip of water.

We all agreed. She might be on the frail side since her dizzy spells became more frequent but compared to most 89-year-olds, Nan was a legend, and Mum and I would be lost without her.

"Eat your peas, Nell," Mum said. "It'll help build your strength up. We don't want you feeling dizzy again, do we?"

Nan rolled her eyes.

"Shall I tell you what I've got for the letter B then?" I continued.

Mum swallowed her chicken at supersonic speed before I had even pursed my lips. "Wait!" she shrieked. "What does your B word sound like?"

"It sounds exactly like what I've got for T," I replied.

"What? Chicken?" Mum asked, lifting the edge of her plate, confused.

"No! Not tea!" I said. "The letter T! I've got twerp for the letter T, which sounds like the word I've got for the letter B. Go on, have a guess. It's really funny!"

"Absolutely not! I think we've all heard quite enough of your alphabet for one night."

I knew my list wouldn't last much longer, but it was fun while it did. Nan wiped both corners of her mouth with a dry hanky she pulled from her raspberry-coloured cardigan, and slowly left the table. She'd barely eaten five mouthfuls.

"Did you get me some pineapple cheese and crackers when you went to the shops today, by any chance?" Nan asked Mum. "You know how partial Sir Barclay is to a cheese and biscuit supper on a Thursday."

"You and that parrot, honestly! He costs us a fortune! The

cheese is in the fridge, but I could only find olive crackers this week. Are you sure he can't eat seeds and nuts like any other bird?"

And that is one of the many reasons why I hate birds. Not because Sir Barclay doesn't eat nuts or seeds, but because Nan's treasured parrot thinks he owns the place, and he doesn't.

He's a rude, uppity, scrunch-bag who randomly flew into Nan's attic-room last year and since then, has completely taken over. She won't hear a bad word said against him because she's convinced he was a sign from Grandpa Willie, 'sent from the grave', whatever that means.

But I know Sir Barclay is the one behind our disappearing chess pieces, and it's only a matter of time before I can prove it.

"Seeds and nuts?" Nan replied curtly. "Certainly not! Only the finest food will do for my Sir Barclay."

That bird! How had he managed to wrap Nan around his little wing after only twelve months?

"I'll try a different shop tomorrow then," Mum offered while she cleared the plates.

"Thank you. Now, if you'll excuse me, I'm going to head up for a rest. That beautiful tea you cooked us has put me in need of a sit down." She patted her tummy.

Nan waited for Mum to fetch the cheese from the fridge and take the plates through to the kitchen before winking at me through her half-mooned spectacles.

"It's not your poor mum's fault she can't cook a good Caribbean dish. Your father obviously didn't listen to me properly!" she whispered. "I've got six chocolate biscuits, two packets of crisps, and a pot of peanuts under my armchair for us to share. Much better than tonight's cremated mash!"

Nan shuffled out of the dining room towards the stairs with Sir Barclay's cheese tucked under her arm.

Strangely, she was wearing only one green slipper.

# CHAPTER TWO

## *Sir Barclay Wigbert Titus Smythe*

The school gates were always pandemonium at the end of the day, and today was no different. I quickly made my way through the queues of gossiping parents and barking dogs, only to find Ruby and Anais waiting at the school entrance. It still felt weird not hanging out together. Ruby spotted me and made a quick snoring noise at Anais before turning away. It was only a faint snore, but I heard it all the same.

"Are you two up to anything fun tonight?" I asked cautiously.

They might feel differently towards me at the moment, but I haven't changed. I still want us to be friends.

"Yes, thanks!" Anais swished her long, ginger hair away from her pink lip gloss.

Ruby remained glued to her text messages. "What's it to you?" She slid her thick rimmed glasses further up her nose.

I nervously scratched my thumbnail, but Ruby didn't even look up from her phone. I got that they ignored me when Celeste was around, that they were itching to impress her, but to be this cold and unfriendly on their own was something new.

"No reason," I said, desperately trying not to sound desperate. "Just wondered."

A huge, brand-spanking-new 4x4 appeared in front of us, bringing with it the scent of warm rubber wafting from its equally enormous tyres.

"Thanks for waiting!" Celeste called from the back window that she had fully opened so she could hang out of it and wave like some sort of celebrity. "Mum had parked two streets away, so I figured it was easier to direct her right up to the gates."

I couldn't see Celeste's mum, but I presumed it was she who had turned up the car radio, which was blasting out the news. "Police today refused to comment on whether they had made further developments on the recent sightings of flesh-like objects in the sky. To date, two hands and a leg have been witnessed flying around the local area. Unofficial sources claim the police are not ruling out links to the separate findings of one green and one purple slipper. This evening's weather. . . "

"Come on then girls. Hop in!" Celeste said.

Ruby immediately slipped her phone into her pocket and jumped straight into the front seat.

Anais knocked my shoulder with hers as she clambered to join the others in the car. I bit my lip to stop it from trembling. I wasn't in her way. She had plenty of room and could've easily walked past without pushing.

"Midweek cinema trip and pasta here we come!" Celeste scoffed loudly, glaring at me before popping on a large pair of sunglasses.

It was like I was wearing a sign that read: 'Don't Come Anywhere Near Me'.

She rolled up the car window and it whizzed off down the road.

BANG!

I slammed the front door open after running as fast as my long, skinny legs would take me. Away from school and away from them. Another flake of cherry-red paint dropped to the floor from the door-handle-shaped dent I had created behind it. I didn't mean to slam it so hard.

I seemed to be wound up a lot lately. Especially when the school bell chimed at the end of the day, because I couldn't wait to escape the mean giggles and whispers and snores between Celeste 'The Best' and her two sidekicks.

After they drove off, I raced home via Farrow Park and without getting attacked by its army of swooping, pooping pigeons. I made it back in nine minutes flat. Pretty impressive, I'd say, given my full bladder and a near-miss with a Honda Jazz outside.

I heeled off my school pumps and legged it upstairs for a wee.

"Is that you, Cindy?"

"No, Nan, it's me," I shouted from the toilet.

"What are you doing here so early? Didn't you want to hang around with your friends after school and make the playground look untidy, like me and your grandpa used to?"

Nan mentions Grandpa Willie every day. What he would

make of the bin strike and the temporary traffic lights down the road. What he used to like for lunch (not Mum's soup that's for sure!). We all missed him. Such a lot had changed in the last year that it was hard to believe it hadn't been longer.

"Not today," I replied as I angrily hurled the hand towel into the empty bath before climbing up to the third floor. We might not live in the biggest end-terrace you've ever seen but judging by how fast my breathing gets when I reach the top, it certainly feels like the tallest.

Nan had been adamant she was fit and healthy enough for our spare attic-room when she sold her flat. Her legs still had bags of life in them apparently and she didn't want Mum or I to be uprooted from our bedrooms simply because she was moving in. Something about needing the best views, and the exercise to keep her young.

I knocked on the door then walked straight in, to be greeted as always with one of Nan's infectiously warm smiles. My breathing levelled and I felt calmer already.

Nan's room was incredible with a chosen place for everything. Every nook and cranny brimmed with photos, trinkets, and baskets containing more trinkets! Houseplants spilled over colourful pots next to her armchair. Bright, thick leaves tickled the ceiling as the smaller plants nestled inside the shelves that surrounded her cosy window in the middle of the wall.

I had helped Mum paint two walls blue and the other two white before Nan moved in. She arrived a couple of days later with a thick pair of yellow curtains and some matching blue, white, and yellow cushions that filled the room with life. It was a bit like being on a beach only without the sand, particularly as a vibrant canvas of St. Lucia proudly occupied the space behind her bed.

Nan took a break from writing in her reddy-orangey notebook beside the window to ask, "Why not, baby?"

Sir Barclay straightened his back and glared at me as I tried to think up a convincing excuse. What could Nan do about it anyway?

"I just didn't feel like playing tonight, that's all." I scratched the little rice-crispie-sized mole on my left cheek. "And I was bursting for the toilet." Technically that part wasn't a lie.

"Well then, that makes two of us." She smiled. "Be a love and put the kettle on for me, would you? I'll spend a quick penny myself then we can finish our game of chess before your mum gets home and gives us both a grilling for you not doing your homework."

"Deal!" I said. Nan and I swapped places and she left the room humming.

I flicked the switch on the kettle which bubbled loudly, much to the annoyance of Sir Barclay, who glared at me and twitched his plump chest at being disturbed. Fluffy, grey layers of white-tipped feathers overlapped each other around his neck as the kettle continued to boil. His sharp, needle-like nails scratched the perch as he turned away and blatantly flashed me his bottom. Clearly pleased with his efforts, he then flapped back around to resume his glaring position.

Ugh! Did I mention I hate birds? Every last one of them. Well, apart from penguins because they're cute and technically can't fly. How amazing would it be to fly? If I found out I could fly, I'd be off. Celeste 'The Best' wouldn't see me for dust. I'd head straight to St. Lucia to see where Nan was born and soak up some sun. I'd still hate birds though–especially the ones that attacked me in Farrow Park last week.

I've been working on my 'top five most horrible and annoying birds' list for ages and I think I perfected it yesterday.

5. Cockerels. Too loud.
4. Geese. Too spitty.
3. Seagulls. Too greedy.
2. Pigeons. Too flappy.
1. Sir Barclay. Too annoying. I could fill an entire notebook with his annoying habits.

What kind of name is that for a parrot anyway? I once asked Nan why she named him Sir Barclay, and she said that was the name he appeared with. When he randomly perched his pompous bottom on her windowsill the day before Grandpa Willie's funeral, a little, metal name tag dangled around his neck that read Sir Barclay Wigbert Titus Smythe.

Yes, that's right. Sir Barclay Wigbert Titus Smythe. Who does he think he is? Royalty? He might like to strut around like he's some sort of king, but I'm not falling for it. In my opinion he's nothing more than a lumpy, grumpy, chess-pinching feather-face.

I tried to ignore the pesky parrot, choosing instead to sit on the stool opposite Nan's comfy green armchair to study where we had left our game before school earlier.

The chain flushed. Nan wasn't as nimble on her feet these days, so I knew I had a good few minutes to make her tea before she was back in the room with us. I heard Sir Barclay shuffle and felt his eyeballs attacking my face. Why did he always have to stare at me? Ever since he arrived it was like he didn't want anything to do with me, which was fine, as I didn't want anything to do with him either. His rudeness made my blood boil faster than Nan's steaming kettle.

Without thinking, I snapped, "What is your problem, you ugly, little bird? You're not going to put me off my chess moves this time. I don't know what you're up to, Sir Feather Bum,"–I wielded one of Nan's teaspoons in his direction–"but any more of your chess-piece-pinching funny business, and I'll make sure the window is locked good and proper the next time you nip out for a night flap!"

"*Squawk!*" Sir Barclay replied.

Good. That had rattled him.

"*Squawk!*"

I could tell he wasn't happy with me as he had started to flap his feathers and dip his shoulders.

"Shh, keep your voice down," I said, as I poured hot water into Nan's mug. "I won't hurt you, not really. Although I hear African Grey parrot-feathers make the softest cushions." I giggled to myself as I squeezed out the teabag.

"*SQUAWK!*"

Okay, perhaps I had gone a little further than I intended with my tormenting, but he deserved it. Twelve months I had put up with his rudeness. If you asked me, someone needed to teach him a lesson.

"Don't worry, Sir Barclay," Nan chirruped reassuringly from the door. "I'm almost back."

I could hear Nan gasping for breath at the top of the stairs.

"*Squawk!* You touch one feather on my head, Miss Fleur 'You-Can't-Play-Chess-for-Toffee' Marie, and I'll pinch your king this time, as well as your rook and your queen and your bishop. *Squawk!*"

I dropped the teabag and gasped. That didn't just happen, did it? I was hearing things. Surely, I must have been hearing things. My hands shook and went cold. Sir Barclay didn't really just say that out loud, did he?

Nan once managed to get Sir Barclay to say, "I'm the finest reflection you'll ever meet!" but that was it. She had certainly never taught him to say anything else.

"Here I am," Nan said. "Now then, what have I missed?

# CHAPTER THREE

## *Birdrobe*

I never lost all my chess games to Nan until tonight. At first, I thought I was distracted by the corks we were using as replacement pieces, but they hadn't put me off before. The only reason Nan and I started using replacement chess pieces in the first place was because so many of our original pieces had disappeared.

Our latest brainwave of labelling corks was fine and functional in the beginning, when only one or two pieces were missing, but the number of corks had fast overtaken the number of traditional chess pieces we now had. At this rate our board would soon resemble a wine cellar, and Nan would still probably thrash me.

There was nothing I could do about it. What made it even worse was having Sir Barclay stare at me from his perch the entire time, sporting a humongous smirk.

"Everything all right, baby?" Nan whipped my prized queen away with her pawn, seconds into our third game. "It's not like you to make silly mistakes or have you decided to give your old Nan a fighting chance at winning a full house for once?"

I wish. I couldn't focus on our game. I couldn't focus on anything apart from what I thought I'd heard before the game. And I had heard him. Hadn't I? Unless the radio was on. Although I didn't think Nan was listening to anything when I came up to her room. It had to be Sir Barclay, didn't it? It did. It was. He had spoken to me. There was no mistaking it.

How was it possible that I could hear Sir Barclay talk now, when I'd never heard him before?

"Checkmate." Nan had acquired all my whites mixed with a couple of cork pieces too. "Fancy one more for the road? I think I'm on a roll!"

"Do you mind if we call it a night?" I said. "I think I could do with an early one. It's been a long day."

Nan cupped my face and rubbed her thumb up and down my cheek. "Of course, I don't mind. Just promise me that you'll tell me if anything's bothering you, won't you? You've got a lot going on with this being your last term before high school."

I knew the calm in my head wouldn't last long. Maybe the silver lining to learning Sir Barclay could talk, meant that I was able to worry about something other than Celeste, Ruby, and Anais for a change. That was until Nan mentioned school.

"I will," I lied. "But everything's fine, I promise." I crossed my fingers behind my back, praying for forgiveness if Nan ever found out I'd been untruthful to her. "I'm just tired, that's all. We had double-maths today, so I must've used up all my concentration reserves."

Nan nodded in agreement and twisted her earring. "Just like your father. He had to think properly when it came to maths too! Sleep tight, baby."

"Night, Nan. See you in the morning."

"*Squawk!* Night, night, chess loser! *Squawk!* Sweet dreams!"

My heart jumped. It caused an uncontrollable squeal to escape my mouth, which made my legs dither and knock me into the end of Nan's bed. I shot Nan a worried look as I scanned back and forth between her and Sir Barclay, flustered and confused.

"Fleur! My goodness! Are you okay?" Nan pulled herself up from her chair.

"Did you hear that?"

"Hear what, baby?"

My eyes flickered towards Sir Barclay who twitched his head and flew towards the perch in the far corner of his cage, seemingly delighted with my reaction.

"Nothing," I replied, quickly backing out of the room. "Must've been something outside. Told you I was tired."

Nan raised her eyebrows towards me then across at the annoying waft of feathers snuggled in the corner. She sat back down with an electric glint in her eye but when I blinked, she was just staring at me with concern.

I had been wide awake since 4am. My shin was throbbing, and I couldn't sleep, not even for five minutes, which is unheard of. Usually, I sleep like a log after a bath and a couple of chapters of my favourite book, but not last night, not after what happened between me and Sir Barclay.

Mum has always joked that I can sleep through anything. She was once so worried when she couldn't wake me, that she switched the vacuum cleaner on right next to my head to make sure I was still alive.

Only last night was different. I was more like a jack-in-the-box or a dolphin. Did you know that dolphins rarely sleep? And if they do, only half their brain shuts down, which means the other half is wide awake. Well, that was me all night, unable to sleep properly, and restless from the minute my head hit the pillow.

I hadn't a clue what was going on outside, but it was exhausting. If it wasn't annoying birds twittering outside my open window or tapping their beaks against the glass, it was what sounded like a million voices drifting through the night. People chatting, dogs barking, cats screeching. If I didn't know any better, I'd say Sir Barclay put them all up to it for fun just to stop me from having any shuteye.

"Come on, Fleur! Shake a leg! If you don't hurry up this porridge will be stone cold."

It was good to know at least Mum had enjoyed a full night's rest.

"Coming." I yawned as I slowly began my morning routine which, coincidentally, I've condensed into six very simple steps:

1. Shower and dress.
2. Shove curly, big hair into plaits.
3. Eat breakfast (if Mum's made her vile porridge, then hold breath to eat it).
4. Tray to Nan (if Mum's made her vile porridge, tell Nan to hold breath too).
5. Brush teeth.
6. Shoes on and away.

At best, I'd say it takes me eleven minutes, leaving me plenty of time to walk through Farrow Park and into school without looking like a sweaty frizz-ball, and before the bell rings. Winner.

"There you are." Mum plonked a kiss on my head as I sat down at the dining table. "I thought I was going to have to use a bucket of water to bring you around this morning."

"Why? Did you think it would be better than using the vacuum cleaner this time?" I had the world's biggest stretch before gingerly testing the temperature of the porridge against my tongue to make sure it wasn't too hot.

"Bit of a smarty-pants are we this morning? You're just like your dad, that's the kind of thing he would say." Mum smiled sadly before shaking her head and reaching for the fruit bowl. "Here then, you'd best chop this into your breakfast to fuel that enormous, smarty-pants brain of yours." She threw me a banana.

"I'm alright, thanks," I said, catching it. "Not hungry today–porridge is fine."

"Are you alright, love? You're not yourself lately. Is everything okay at school?"

You mean apart from the fact that Celeste 'The Best' looks at me like something she's trodden on, uses me as a verbal punchbag, enjoys battering my ankles during hockey practice, and–oh yeah, finding out I CAN HEAR SIR BARCLAY TALK?!

I somehow managed to control my breathing and slowly stirred my porridge.

"Everything's fine, Mum," I lied. I was getting good at this now.

"As long as you're sure?"

I nodded. This lying business was draining but I had managed to keep her off the scent again.

"Is Nan's ready?" I asked, before finishing my last spoonful. "I'll go and see if it's to her taste, if so."

"It'll be the first time in twelve months if it is!" Mum said jokingly, as she spooned the gloopy porridge into a bowl and placed it on Nan's tray.

Poor Nan. It must feel strange for her living with us after a lifetime with Grandpa Willie, but we're much better for her than a care home. She knows it deep down, but I guess it doesn't stop her from missing him. I miss him too. And Dad, but that's different. Dad isn't dead. He's just gone away for a bit to clear his head after the shock of losing Grandpa Willie. Only no one told me clearing his head meant he would be gone for months and months with no phone call or anything.

Grandpa Willie was 'Porridge Maker Extraordinaire' as Nan tells us every morning. Which basically means Mum isn't, but she keeps on trying. Anything to keep Nan happy and her mind off Dad, who still hasn't phoned her back like he said he would.

"Morning, Nan!" I beamed, opening her bedroom door with my foot. "Meals on wheels, at your service."

"*Squawk!* Ooh yummy, another bowl of grey, lumpy slop. I bet she can hardly wait. *Squawk!*"

My stomach tightened. I hadn't imagined things yesterday, then. It hadn't all been some dreadful daydream.

"*Squawk!* You're very quiet. Did you think I was all in your head? Sorry to disappoint you. *Squawk!*"

I'm pretty sure he would be quiet if he was suddenly faced

with a know-it-all talking parrot and no idea how or why it had happened. Surely this was odd for him too, unless he could flap around and chat to anyone he fancied. And if he could, would they even be able to understand him anyway? None of it made any sense.

"Well. . . I. . . err. . . I don't know," I said, swallowing a large lump in my throat. "Where's Nan?"

Nan's bedcovers were all neat and tidy, and her teacup was empty except for one last sip, which she always left out of politeness. There was no sign of her anywhere.

"*Squawk!* It's secret business. What's it to you?"

The nerve of the bird! How rude! Of course, it's my business. She's my nan not his.

"Do you talk to everyone like this?" I snapped.

"I should be so lucky. Months I've waited for your nan to find someone who can hear and understand me. Months! *Squawk!* And who do I find out has the precious gift of Animalation? You! Fleur Marie Bottom. Marvellous. You don't know your bishops from your pawns, so what chance have I got in finding Dame Genevieve now?"

"Animalation? Special gifts? What are you on about?"

"Precisely my point; you don't understand. You'll never understand. All the watching your nan has done, all the writing everything down in her book, and for what? I'm back to square one."

"What book? What gifts? Just tell me what's going on. I'm not a mind reader!"

I placed the tray of tepid porridge on Nan's chest of drawers and walked over to her wardrobes. Yes, that's right. Wardrobes. Nan's got four of them. All lined up against the back wall, in a dark wood that's very old-fashioned–perfect for nans all over the world–complete with gold, dangly handles and the odd woodworm hole too.

Nan only kept a few bits in the smallest, thinnest one at the end which she'd filled with a large, red, leather suitcase and a couple of coats.

The other wardrobes, where Nan used to keep her clothes, were opened out for her pompous fluff-ball, now perched directly opposite me. Nan had somehow taken the doors off, squeezed all her clothes into her drawers, and attached several garden canes from one side to the other. It offered him a range of perches to choose from and was the grandest birdcage I had ever seen. Instead of being a wardrobe for clothes, it had become a Birdrobe for Sir Barclay.

I had zero clue what all this special gift or Animalation twaddle was about. Nan was missing, and the clock was ticking closer towards the school bell. This meant I was closer to having to face Celeste 'The Best' and another round of her horribleness.

I felt my eyes prickle but I tried my hardest not to cry in front of Sir Barclay. What did it all mean? How could I hear him all of a sudden? Could Nan hear him too? She definitely gave me a funny look last night before bed. And what about Mum? Maybe she knew something too.

Sir Barclay pointed his shiny beak towards the ceiling with an air of superiority.

"Okay, so, you're not in my head. Congratulations. Now what?"

"*Squawk!* How should I know?" he replied. "It's a shock for me as well."

Getting answers to any of my questions from this stubborn parrot felt impossible.

"Look, we've all got to live under the same roof. Can't we at least try to get along nicely? Figure this out together? I've got enough going on at school without your tailfeathers making things worse."

"Forget it!" he snapped. "Your nan can't help me, and neither can you. I'll have to carry on searching for an older, more mature Animalator. Someone capable of handling the ability to hear and understand all animals. Forget I said anything."

"Wait. What do you mean *all* animals?" I asked Sir Barclay.

"I should like to see you try telling your nan or your mum that I spoke to you," Sir Barclay said, ignoring my question. "Who would ever believe you, anyway? You've had a chat with a talking parrot! I've never heard anything so ridiculous in all my life."

It wasn't that ridiculous. People talk to their pets all the time, the difference being they don't usually talk back. Sir Barclay had a point though, who would believe me? I still didn't understand how it had suddenly switched on. My head was fizzing, as in full-scale, both sides of a dolphin's brain awake. Did he really mean all animals?

A strong breeze suddenly rattled the clasp of Nan's window then blasted between me and Sir Barclay. It immediately stopped our conversation and my animals thoughts.

"Aaagh! Nan!"

I completely froze. My stomach lurched but it had nothing to do with Mum's porridge. It was Nan. Sitting there, fully dressed, in her armchair, wearing one green and one purple slipper. She scrutinised my, and Sir Barclay's, every move as she battled with her breakfast. It was so weird because one second, she wasn't in the room, and now, there she was.

"What's up with Sir Barclay?" Nan asked, her eyes not leaving mine.

"Oh, err. . . nothing. I was just saying goodbye before school."

"Hmm." She dropped her lingering gaze to scowl at her spoon instead.

"Ugh, I can't eat this muck. Tell your mum thank you but to try a bit less milk tomorrow. Maybe add some honey and dried papaya. That ought to give it a bit of a boost."

Nan lifted her elbow and reached for another tissue squirreled away inside her sleeve, and that's when I saw it. Sir Barclay was right. He mentioned she wrote a lot of stuff down, and I was ashamed to admit that I hadn't really noticed before, but I was becoming more curious by the second. I was itching to know what was inside the tired, reddy-orangey book nestled between Nan's thigh and the inside of the armrest.

# CHAPTER FOUR

## *Fruity Biscuits*

Ding-a-ding-dong-ding-a-ding-dong-ding-a-ding-DONG!

The school bell chimed its annoying panpipe tune across the playground, the sound wriggling its way into my ears like spaghetti and making my tummy feel all knotty. I do like school, just not everyone there. Well, mainly one person—Celeste—who unluckily for me, stood outside our classroom door with Anais and Ruby as I approached.

"Here she is!" Celeste announced. Celeste was small and dainty with perfectly groomed black hair which glistened as brightly as her perfectly straight teeth. "We were just talking about you."

I was instantly on edge, particularly as her voice notched up a volume. It grabbed the attention of everyone around her, which today was a combination of our Year Six class and a few over-eager Year Fives, who were keen to fill our shoes when we left Buxworth Primary School in less than two weeks' time.

Two weeks—can you imagine that? I do. All the time. No more constant Celeste. It's the only thing getting me through.

"Oh, I love what you've done with your hair this morning,

Fleur. It's beautiful," Celeste went on sarcastically. "Tell me, have you added red streaks on purpose, or did the pigeons eat too many berries for breakfast today?"

I delicately touched the top of my head to check for any 'very berry' bird poo–it wouldn't be the first time one of them had timed their early morning bottom-splat to land on my parting with precision. They always flapped around me. It was like they could sense something I couldn't. Everyone gawped as I investigated. Phew, it was clear.

Celeste laughed, prompting those who hadn't yet entered their own classrooms to copy her and cackle before doing so. It was such a lame joke. I suspected Anais and Ruby felt the same too because, even though they laughed, they avoided eye contact with me and shuffled their feet awkwardly instead.

Why did she always pick on me?

"You know you've got feathers on your jumper though, right?" Celeste continued.

Anais gently shook her head at me which I almost missed, but she stopped when Celeste shot her an icy glare. Something felt off. Celeste was up to something.

I tried to exit the playground, walk down the ramp and into my classroom. After talking parrots, suspicious Nans, and a mysterious notebook, all I wanted was for everything to go back to normal, only now Celeste blocked my path and stopped me walking towards the door.

I moved to the right. She moved too. I moved to the left. So did she.

"She's going to have to do better than that!" came a voice from above.

I looked up to see what was going on but could only

spot a dozen or so birds circling my head, with another six neatly perched along the guttering; their beady eyes all on me.

"She needs faster footwork!" someone else shouted. "I thought you said she was the special one. She doesn't look very special to me!"

What was going on? I could hear voices everywhere, but there was only me, Celeste, Ruby, and Anais left in the playground.

"We don't want her feet to move too fast!" said another voice. "Some of us want to avoid being squashed to smithereens!"

I looked everywhere–along the walls, down the path, but all I could see was a busy line of ants trailing away from my shoe and onto a rogue dandelion near the drain.

"What's she looking for?" I heard Anais whisper to Ruby, who shrugged, bewildered.

More birds appeared–blackbirds, pigeons, starlings, all vigorously flapping their wings and chirping excitedly. I tried to ignore them, but it was exactly how they started before they mobbed me in Farrow Park.

Celeste peered around, enthralled by the commotion. "They like you, don't they, Fleur?" she asked.

"What? No, they don't."

Could she feel it too? That we were being watched? That we were surrounded by mysterious voices?

"Don't be embarrassed, Fleur. I can see these birds have got a real soft spot for you." Celeste's lips curled into an enormous smirk that made me want to throw up.

"This doesn't look good, does it, lads?" said a voice.

"No," replied another. "But I smell food. Can you smell food?"

My mouth gaped dumbstruck, as three large magpies appeared to have a conversation above my head about me, whilst attempting to predict my next move. I put my fingers in my ears and closed my eyes.

"La la la!" I tried to block everything out.

This wasn't right. Just as last night with Sir Barclay wasn't right. It was creepy and disturbing, and it was stressing me out. I opened my eyes to see Ruby and Anais frowning at me behind Celeste who continued to smirk. I moved my hands to my hips and took a deep breath. There had to be a rational explanation for it all. An open window somewhere perhaps, with someone leaning out and offering this ridiculous minute-by-minute commentary.

This was it. Panic was going off inside my head like an alarm clock, or the world's loudest panpipes. I could feel the blood swishing and swirling around my body as I tried to second-guess what she was going to do next. Whatever it was, I knew I wasn't going to like it–I never did.

Anais and Ruby giggled. Of the three of us, why had Celeste chosen to pick on me? How was I any different to Ruby or Anais?

"Look," I said, trying to squeeze past. "I'm going inside before Mr Augustus comes out and tells us off for being late."

"Wait!" Celeste yelled as she pushed me back, this time leaving Ruby and Anais to corner me. "We can't go yet, can we, girls? Not until we've fed Fleur's lovely birds."

"They're not my b-birds!" I stuttered nervously.

It didn't take a genius to work out I hated birds, but Celeste was making me too anxious to explain. If only she realised, I didn't have a clue why they pooed, or flapped, or pecked my head whenever they got the chance. It was as though they sensed I didn't like them.

"Don't worry, I've got something special that I'm sure they'll enjoy."

Celeste pulled a packet of fruity biscuits out of her pocket. I could see her squashing both biscuits inside the packet, turning two fruity rounds into a bag of crumbs.

"Told you I sensed food," a magpie said.

"Did somebody say food? Food? Where is it?" Tweets, chirps, and thrilled voices erupted everywhere.

I wanted to put my fingers in my ears again and shut it all off.

"This isn't going to end well, is it, Legs?" came a different voice.

I still couldn't figure out where all the voices were coming from. There were so many.

"Nope, Shell," said another. "Her with the plaits could do with getting a shift on though, couldn't she? Oi! You with plaits! Get a shift on!"

"Her with the plaits?" I said, alarmed. "That's me!" I spun around, unsure who had tipped me off.

"Err yeah, we know you've got plaits," Ruby said frowning, still not letting me past.

I fixed on Celeste who had already opened the packet of crumbs and was mid-launch in my direction. I finally twigged what she was up to. I tried to dart away from them by scrabbling under a wooden flower box which lined the wall to our classroom door.

A large snail oozed its glue next to my head and stuck tightly to the wood which had offered slight protection. A silvery spider crawled over the top of its shell.

"Could've been worse!" the spider said, making me jump as I felt crumbs slide down my neck and into my polo shirt, and wedge within my plaits. "Could've been the whole packet."

"Ow!" I squealed, as I hit my head against the flower box in utter shock at hearing the spider's upbeat observations.

This was crazy! I was clearly going mad. Unless this was what Sir Barclay meant when he said '*all* animals' last night?

I started to shake the crumbs off when what felt like an army of pigeons, sparrows, magpies, and blackbirds all darted towards me at bird-flapping speed from the nearby trees and guttering. Dozens of wings and pecking beaks were beating my head and shoulders as they fought to steal a crumb and, if they were really lucky, a raisin too.

"Aaagh!" I screamed. "Shoo! Get away, you horrible things!"

"Can't you stop them?" Celeste laughed. "What a waste!"

A waste of biscuits? A waste of time? What was she on about? Their mouths dropped, and Anais and Ruby stepped away as the birds continued to feast on my biscuit head. Eventually, my demented shooing saw them off. Celeste simply turned and skipped into the classroom, pulling Ruby and Anais inside with her.

A large teardrop formed in my eye and slowly rolled down my cheek before getting stuck on a rogue biscuit crumb. I didn't understand. Why wouldn't Celeste leave me alone?

"Told you I didn't like the look of it, didn't I?' whispered a bird, until a parrot-shaped shadow suddenly appeared, forcing the birds to separate, and the snail and spider to freeze in terror.

A packet of tissues fell from the sky and landed at my feet.

"*Squawk!* And what exactly are you going to do now? *Squawk!*"

I felt marginally better by lunchtime. Immediately after Mr Augustus called my name from the register, I went to the toilets and managed to pick out most of the feathers and crumbs from my plaits.

A large clump of wet, paper towels sorted out the leftover marks on my jumper, which was enough to stop people getting wind of anything strange. I only wished Sir Barclay hadn't seen everything. What was he even doing flying over my school anyway? He'd never done that before. He was probably at home now thinking I was the world's biggest wimp for not standing up to Celeste or telling Mr Augustus the real reason why I turned up late.

I've wondered the same thing myself, which probably confirms that I am the world's biggest wimp, but with only two weeks left of term, why make things even worse?

The rest of my morning was spent avoiding Celeste. The only thing that perked me up was remembering it was cheesy pinwheels for lunch. Hot, buttery, swirls of pastry, smothered in salty cheese, which are my absolute favourite unless, of course, they're made by Mum.

Today's school cheesy pinwheels were delicious and I savoured every mouthful. Until Celeste, Ruby, and Anais strangely plonked their trays down on the space next to me.

"Anyone sat here, Feather Face?" Celeste was still smirking about earlier.

I could feel the smugness radiating from her face. Celeste didn't wait for me to answer. She never waited for anyone to answer, preferring instead to bluster her way through school life however she pleased.

"Pudding, Fleur?" It was Mrs Sponge who was in charge of the school dessert trolley.

"No, thanks," I said.

I could easily have squeezed in a portion of apple cake and custard but being surrounded by Celeste and the others had knocked my appetite. I needed to get to the library before the blue, water jug 'accidentally' fell in my lap or the salt 'suddenly' leapt up my left nostril.

"Here, love, take these with you." Mrs Sponge handed me two packets of flapjacks. "You'll need these to build your strength up, so you're fit and ready for hockey practice tomorrow morning. It is tomorrow, isn't it?" she asked the four of us, assuming we were all friends.

Celeste smiled sweetly at Mrs Sponge as she always did, while Ruby and Anais attempted to copy her, and failed, both looking stiff and uncomfortable.

Celeste on the other hand was the queen of smiling sweetly. It's how she manages to fool people into thinking that she's nicer than she is. She loves nothing more than to pretend she wouldn't hurt a fly, while she makes everything that happens to me appear like an 'accident', or in some way my fault. It basically means she can get away with being unkind and avoid detection.

"Yes, it is!" Celeste said. "And we're really looking forward to playing nicely together–aren't we, Fleur?"

Hmmm. Let me think about that for a minute. . . NO!

Ruby and Anais joined the queue for the salad bar, leaving me alone with Celeste. My earlier efforts to dodge her were now futile. I tightly clutched my tray, ready to stand up, when Celeste leaned close to me. Any closer and she would have been able to hear the thumping in my ears as well.

"Wonder if any animals will help you out tomorrow?" she whispered.

My ears pounded so hard it felt like they would blast away from my head at any moment. Why would Celeste suddenly mention animals and what did she know? I gripped my tray tighter but didn't move an inch. She was on to me.

# CHAPTER FIVE

## *Three-Bean Bouyon*

This is how it all began or rather ended. You see, I wasn't always the odd one out. Far from it, and up until three months ago, you would have found me happily playing with Ruby and Anais in the library, as we had done since we were five. We weren't in the cool gang like some other girls in our class, but that didn't bother us one bit because we had each other, and we liked the fact that we had a different type of coolness from everyone else.

We were quite happy doing our own thing without hurting anyone. I mostly liked to read but had taught both Ruby and Anais to play chess, and between us we were getting pretty good and growing more competitive.

Ruby is the fastest learner because her head is naturally wired to solving puzzles. It doesn't have to be a boardgame, any type of puzzle will do–Sudoku, jigsaws, you name it.

Anais is a different character altogether. She's less puzzle-based and more artistic–she draws incredible pictures, totally freehand.

Anyway that was us; three best friends who shared a

love of books, chess, jigsaws, and drawing, and happy just the way we were. Until, of course, the day the new girl appeared.

"Oh, my days, call this a library? It's tiny!" The loud, posh voice invaded our quiet space near the window.

I didn't look up from my book at first but could see from the corners of my eyes that Anais had stopped sketching her elephant, and Ruby had paused trying to find jigsaw pieces that resembled UK landmarks.

"The library at my last school was enormous! It was almost the same size as your school hall. And it was full of brand new books, not like these shabby, scrappy ones. I mean, look at this—I bet it's older than my grandpa." She placed a dog-eared copy of *Carrie's War* back on the dusty rack and walked along to the next row.

Ruby and Anais smiled at each other as the new girl moved a single strand of her black hair back to its neatly groomed position.

"Look at the first page with all the publishing information on it," I said. "That'll tell you how old it is."

I wasn't being difficult, simply stating a fact. One which she chose to scoff at and ignore.

She paced along the shelves, tutting, and scrunching her nose in disgust, particularly when she saw the beanbags in the far corner. They weren't the cleanest, but then they wouldn't be—they'd had 180-plus children sitting on them at various times during the week.

"Come to think of it, I think my grandpa would fit in perfectly with you lot; it's similar to his nursing home. I mean, no offence or anything." (Which in my opinion is what people say just before they're about to offend you). "But it's a bit dull in here, isn't it?"

Boom. There it was. I put my book down. I didn't know who this girl was barging in here, criticising our library and our hobbies, but I was pretty sure that I didn't like her already. She walked back along the shelves towards us and gaped at me in a different way to how she looked at the others. It was cold and suspicious, particularly when she spotted the loose thread and holes on the shoulder of my jumper. It wasn't an old jumper, but Sir Barclay had dug his claws into it when I left it hanging over Nan's chair a few weeks ago. Mum hadn't got around to forking out for a new one yet. I was sure she would soon.

"I'm Celeste, by the way," said the girl. "Celeste Morton."

Ruby and Anais waved, but I decided to hang onto my book a little while longer.

"Do you have a cat?" Celeste asked, pointing at my shoulder.

"Err no," I said, fidgeting with the claw marks trying to cover them up. "My nan's got a parrot, why?"

"Maybe you should have a little word with it sometime, show it who's boss. Or maybe trim its claws."

Celeste was getting ruder and stranger by the minute. What was it to her? I'd have actually loved to show Sir Barclay who was boss, given his overinflated opinion of himself, but I wasn't going to take any hints and tips from someone I barely knew. In any case, don't they say talking to animals is the first sign of madness? I raised my eyebrows and shrugged it off.

"Anyway, don't I know you from somewhere?" Celeste's

frown deepened as she studied my face intently, which was odd. Not to mention unfriendly.

"Not that I know of."

I'm pretty sure I would have remembered her! She looked like she'd stepped straight out of a hair salon and before that the dry cleaners. Her uniform was immaculate. She even had a stiff line ironed into the fabric of her dazzling white shirt, and don't get me started on her hair, which was neatly trimmed into a black bob with a thick, glossy fringe. Worlds apart from my curly locks.

She circled our table, tapping her lips with her fingertip as if trying to wrack her brains. "I'm sure I do," she said firmly. "From a shop, or a park, or something."

"Fleur lives opposite a park," Ruby said. "She can't walk through it without stirring up the animals though. They always find her!"

"Not always!" I said defensively.

"Yes, they do! We've often wondered if she hides packets of dog biscuits or birdseed in her pocket, haven't we, Anais?"

Anais nodded enthusiastically.

"I am still here, thanks," I said, suddenly feeling outnumbered.

I'd been mobbed by an array of pigeons, ducks, squirrels, and sausage dogs on Saturday afternoon come to think of it, but it was none of her business. She wasn't there, and anyway, it wasn't that unusual because animals always follow me around. Birds had never attacked me before Saturday though–and one of them really hurt me. It even made my ear bleed. What can I say? I'm not an animal person, not that it's any of her business.

"You're more than welcome to join us," Ruby said, holding out a pencil and pushing out a spare chair. "I'm Ruby by the way, this is Anais, and that's Fleur."

"I gathered." She continued to glare at me. "Drawing's not really my thing though, thanks. I'm only waiting for the Head to finish his lunch so he can show me around the last few classrooms I haven't seen yet. I'm sure it won't take long though, judging by the size of the place so far."

"Are you moving here, then?" Ruby asked.

"We've already moved. Well, technically this is our sixth move, but five of those were across different parts of France and Italy, so I guess you could say this is more of a relocation."

"That sounds exciting!" Anais's eyes widened. "Are you French? Or Italian?"

"Neither. I was born in the UK. My mum changes jobs a lot, so we all move around together. Whenever she gets promoted, we get to see somewhere new, and Italy was A-MA-ZING! There was one restaurant that made pizza the size of your table!"

"Wow, that sounds fun!" Ruby had now given up on her jigsaw altogether.

"Here, try this," I said, handing her a missing jigsaw piece. Ruby ignored me.

"You only think it sounds fun because you're obsessed with pizza!" Anais added.

"So are you, Anais!" Ruby said crossly. "And don't pretend otherwise!"

I had been shunned into silence. They had forgotten I was there.

"I know, I'm only winding you up–it's too easy!"

Ruby and Anais giggled.

"The furthest I've ever travelled is Scotland, and from memory, I think their pizza tastes the same as the school dinner ones," Ruby said.

Celeste pretended to be sick. "I only eat fresh, stone-baked pizza. I'd never touch one which came out of the freezer. Do you fancy going outside? It's boring in here and these books absolutely stink. I've downloaded some songs we could listen to on my new phone?"

"Yeah, sounds good!" Anais said, standing up. "Are you coming too, Fleur? Be nice to get some fresh air."

"No thanks," I said. "We're fine chilling in here, aren't we?"

I turned to Ruby who suddenly looked at Anais and dodged my gaze.

"That's a shame," Celeste said. "My older brother's playing football outside. He's asked a few of his new friends to tea at our house later. Nothing special, just a couple of Dad's home-made pizzas done in our outside oven. You could join us too if you'd like?"

"Wow! You've got a pizza oven in your garden?" Anais's eyes widened. "That's cool!"

"Of course! Where else would you expect it to be? Mum flew three builders over from Italy to finish it before we moved. You can have any toppings you like, and for dessert, Mum makes pizza with chocolate sauce and marshmallows. They're delicious!"

"I'm afraid I can't tonight," I said. Why would I want to spend time with someone so rude and full of themselves?

Celeste screwed up her eyes. "Do you need permission from your nan's parrot?"

"No! My mum's cooking her three-bean bouyon. It's her day off, and I don't want to let her down. Thanks for the offer, though."

"Ugh, that sounds revolting! What is it?" She shuddered.

I admit it wasn't one of Mum's finer dishes.

"It's basically a bean and vegetable stew," I replied. "It's really nice." Well, it would be if Nan made it.

"Remind me not to sit downwind of you tomorrow then!"

Ruby and Anais sniggered, which wasn't like them.

Nan and I had figured out early on, that when Mum attempted a new recipe, she used fancy or French words to describe otherwise basic dishes. For example, her 'Soup de Crevette' was actually shrimp chowder, 'Tarte au Poisson' was fish pie, and her 'Envelope of Ox' turned out to be a twist on a beef pasty.

Chocolate pizza sounded much more appealing than Mum's windy, three-bean bouyon, but I wasn't going to let the new girl think I was impressed by her.

"What about you two girls? Can you be tempted?"

"We've got stuff to finish here, haven't we?" I said quickly.

"Well, err, it is a bit quiet in here, isn't it, Fleur?" Ruby said. Anais nodded. "And we won't be long. Just ten minutes or so."

Ruby was already packing up her things.

"Yes, just a few minutes so that we can discuss pizza options for tonight!"

"Cool!" Ruby said. "I'll text and ask my mum now."

"Come on, let's go. I'd love to hear more about your drawings, Anais; is that an Asian Elephant? That's fantastic!" Celeste put her hand on Anais's elbow and ushered her towards the door. "And if you like landmarks," she said to Ruby, who was now scurrying after them both, "I can tell you all about the Leaning Tower of Pisa. And hockey! I'll share my best hockey tips with you both because I think you'd both be perfect for the school hockey team. I've already asked the Head if we can set one up as soon as possible."

Celeste smirked back at me, as she held the door open for Ruby and Anais to lead the way. It was at that moment I felt as though I'd lost my best friends forever. Was I being overdramatic? Maybe. But it felt like I had been dropped, with little else to look forward to other than Mum's windy, three-bean bouyon.

# CHAPTER SIX

## *Smashed Ankles*

Most people relish the thought of Friday mornings because it signals the end of the week, the beginning of the weekend, and the start of some fun and relaxation. I used to look forward to them too, but that was months ago. Before Celeste appeared and shook everything up, and now I dread them because Friday mornings equal one thing, and that's hockey.

The last time I checked, there was absolutely nothing fun or relaxing about hockey. The very thought of it makes my skin go weirdly cold and clammy, and my neck feels as though it's being attacked by little pins as every hair on the back of it stands upright in protest. I know it sounds immature and petty, but I honestly think it's the worst sport ever invented, and every Thursday night I pray for a cancellation, but disappointingly it hasn't happened yet.

The only glimmer of positivity on Friday mornings is when the clock ticks over from 11:59am to 12:00pm, and it officially becomes the afternoon, and the sports equipment bag fills up with our hockey gear to be locked away for another blissful week.

I didn't understand what was so wrong with the other sports we had previously enjoyed like badminton, basketball, and rounders, or why Mr Augustus suddenly decided to swap them for one which favoured long sticks with brutally curved ends. I knew exactly who had suggested it though. I overheard her wittering on about it when I was trying to concentrate on my clay model of Queen Victoria.

"Oh, what a shame your school's so behind on promoting pupil independence," Celeste said loudly.

I tried to focus on my model because I didn't want Celeste to think I was bothered about what she was saying, but secretly I listened to every word.

"What do you mean?" Clara leant forward on her elbows along with Ruby, Anais, and a few others.

"What I mean is, when I was in Italy, we were encouraged to have a louder voice."

I raised my eyebrows, which Leena and Suki on my table spotted because they smiled at each other and then at me. I mean, was she joking? As if she needed a louder voice than the one she already had.

"We were always asked our opinions on how we would change things at school," she continued. "You really felt as though you were being listened to and valued. Part of a real democracy, you know?"

Mr Augustus, who was sat at his desk marking homework, suddenly raised his chin and peered at Celeste before beckoning her over to have a chat with him.

And that was it. As part of 'appreciating democracy', our class was then allowed to vote for our preferred sport.

The boys elected football, whereas the girls got lumbered

with hockey–Celeste's favourite sport. She somehow managed to persuade the majority of the girls to choose hockey rather than any of the other, gentler sport, which didn't use sticks that doubled as lethal weapons. So, rain, hail, sun, and snow, I now had the pleasure of having my ankles battered and bruised, all in the name of democracy. Deep joy.

This Friday morning was no different. I even tried to borrow some of Mum's wooden spatulas to put down the sides of my shin pads and socks for extra protection against Celeste, only she and Nan were hovering suspiciously around the kettle.

"What are you doing with those, love?" Mum asked.

Busted. Bottling everything up was fast becoming harder and harder to hide.

"We've been asked to take something wooden in to draw for art this afternoon," I replied. It was a lame excuse, but it was all I could think of on the spot.

"What was that, Fleur? You're doing a spot of cooking at school this afternoon? Does that mean your mum's shrimp chowder is off the menu tonight?" Nan pressed her hands together in prayer, ensuring Mum couldn't see what she was up to, but I wasn't in the mood for laughing today.

"Sorry, Nan, shrimp chowder is still firmly on the menu tonight as I've got art not cooking."

I quickly gathered up my things and hotfooted it out of the kitchen.

"Hang on a minute!" Nan called, as she crept along the hall to meet me at the front door. "If you're really doing wooden art sketching this afternoon, would this help?"

She reached into her lavender cardigan and pulled out

one of our favourite chess pieces which had little bricks and ivy climbing up the side, alongside a castle door. It was a black rook, which was particularly special because Grandpa Willie had hand-carved the whole set himself. We've got a few plain chess sets that we use during the week, and we save Grandpa Willie's for the weekends. Unless some of the pieces go 'missing' and then we either have to mix and match the sets or use labelled corks.

"It's okay thanks, Nan. I've just remembered that school provides us with the wooden stuff, so we don't need to bring our own after all."

"Oh, well then," she said, stuffing the chess piece back inside her cardigan pocket. "I'll hang on to it for later and we can start a new game when you get home from school tonight. What do you think?"

"Sounds good," I said, opening the door to the warm July sunshine which gently kissed my skin. I just had the small matter of hockey practice to get through first.

Mr Augustus reached for his whistle. This was when it got serious: when the whistle no longer bounced around his neck with every enthusiastic teacher step, but instead, was clenched tightly between his teeth, ready for action.

We all had our hockey sticks nervously poised as we hopped from foot to foot, waiting for the whistle to blow. Even the girls on Celeste's team, whom she had personally hand-picked, looked nervous, so you can imagine how the rest of the opposition and I felt. I just wanted to get the game over and done with as quickly as possible, and without injury. Was that too much to ask?

There were twenty-two of us, and only one person had an enormous smile on her face, and it certainly wasn't me.

"Come on, girls! Let's smash this!" Celeste shouted.

I knew deep down she was directing her words of encouragement towards her own team, but playing for the reds against her yellows, my ankles shuddered more than Nan's false teeth on a bumpy bus at the thought of being 'accidentally' hooked or walloped by Celeste's killer, hockey-stick swipe. My ankles had barely recovered from last week, and it wouldn't be long before Mum and Nan started asking questions about my sudden sock obsession in the middle of summer.

The whistle blew and the game started. Celeste 'The Best' was unleashed as she sprinted towards the hockey ball to take control of the game before anyone else got a look in.

"Anais get up front!" she bellowed.

Anais looked like a rabbit trying to dodge an oncoming car, unsure of which direction to go first to avoid danger. Her cheeks flushed pink as her awkward glance met mine because we both sensed she was out of her depth.

After a shimmy to the left, one to the right, then anxiously back to the left again, she finally did as she was told and ran straight ahead. Celeste launched the ball into her path, but before Anais's hockey stick got anywhere near it, Leena Assad from our team flew across the grass and scooped the ball away from her.

"Anais! What are you doing?"

Anais's feet jerked to a stop. "What should I do?" she whispered to me.

I didn't get a chance to reply before Celeste angrily stormed between us to drag the ball back from Leena. This was where it got nasty. It always got nasty as far as Celeste was concerned, and although I felt guilty for thinking it, I couldn't help but feel relieved that it wasn't me she was chasing.

"Come on, Leena!" Beau cheered, as Leena carried on dribbling the ball towards the goal, seconds away from scoring our first team point. Nothing would have given me greater pleasure than to see our reds win against Celeste's yellows, but it hadn't happened so far this year–surely there had to be a first time for everything.

Leena swung her arm back, inches away from making the perfect shot towards the net.

*WHACK!*

Something struck the side of her foot.

"Aaagh!" Leena fell on the muddy grass, clutching her foot in agony.

Celeste didn't waste a second worrying about Leena. She had already turned the ball in the opposite direction, desperate to score a goal for her team, as the rest of us prioritised our teammate, making sure she was okay, and checking for broken bones.

"Goal!" Celeste cheered. "That's 1-0 for the yellows! Good work, girls."

This was outrageous! Where was Mr Augustus when we needed him? I scoured the pitch for evidence of his wig and spotted him smiling and waving in the direction of the staffroom. Ugh. Miss Patsy again. Everyone knew he fancied her.

"What do you mean, good work, girls?" Leena said, holding

her foot and rubbing mud from her knees. She slowly hobbled to her feet. "You cheated! You hit me because you knew I was about to score."

"I'm sorry you slipped, Leena, but there aren't any rules against taking the ball from someone who got stuck in the mud."

"I didn't get stuck in the mud! You knocked me down with your stick! Just like you do every single week to Fleur, or someone else from our team."

Mr Augustus finally spotted the commotion and blew his whistle to stop the heated bickering. "Come on, girls!" he said firmly, jogging across the field clutching his clipboard. "What's going on?"

"She hit my foot to trip me up on purpose and she knows it. That goal should've been ours!"

"Right, come on, settle down. It's just a game."

Was he for real? This hockey tournament was fast becoming more important than the school Christmas performance rehearsals, and they rehearsed for an entire year.

"Everything alright, Celeste?"

"Yes, Mr Augustus! My hand just sort of felt a bit funny, almost numb-ish. It came on ever so suddenly, so I wiggled it a bit to stop the pins and needles, and I don't know. I suppose, perhaps, my stick might've accidentally strayed into Leena's path, but I didn't mean it. It was a total accident."

Mr Augustus watched Celeste, unconvinced, and then scratched his head. "Leena, you swap with Suki for a bit to make sure you've not twisted anything. Celeste, please be more careful. We're building up to the Farrow Park Cup tournament not the Olympics."

"Right you are, Mr A. Yes, of course. Sorry."

Celeste skipped back to the centre of the field, leaving Leena to dejectedly limp over to the benches and recover. How did he keep missing Celeste's devious tactics?

# CHAPTER SEVEN

## *Telling Tales*

The whistle blew and I made a point of sticking tight to my normal place, which is always at least three paces behind everyone else. It doesn't make any difference. She still finds me. Technically, I'm supposed to be a midfielder, but I'm terrible at it. It doesn't matter how hard I try; I never seem able to overcome my fear of getting belted by Celeste, which means I focus too much on defending my ankles than I do the actual game. I wish things could be different.

The ball was heading towards me, along with a stampede of classmates wielding sticks, and wearing red and yellow bibs which ballooned at speed. They looked like a human game of Connect 4, only less neat, and led by Celeste's sweaty face which was morphing into the colour of a beetroot. No wonder really. It was baking hot without a cloud in the sky, which made the game more brutal than ever.

*WHOOSH!*

A fierce gust of wind slapped our faces, forcing my plaits to whip the opposite sides of my cheeks. A large, empty packet of prawn cocktail crisps had somehow glued itself to

Celeste's forehead with the force of the wind and covered her eyes. She couldn't see a thing, and the packet refused to budge, despite her attempts to pull it off.

Suki seized Celeste's sudden sight impairment as the perfect opportunity to effortlessly slog the ball back towards our goal at the opposite end of the field. Within seconds, Suki had passed to Jasmine, Jasmine passed to Emi, and before we knew it, Beau had tapped the ball between Ruby's legs to secure an even point.

"One-all!" Mr Augustus shouted. "Great teamwork, girls, keep it up!"

Celeste finally managed to yank the crisp packet from her eyes and angrily threw it to the ground before marching up to the centre of the pitch where she waited for the whistle.

Mr Augustus didn't hang about, and Celeste was off. She wasted no time in getting stuck in. Within seconds, she had elbowed Lydia, stamped on Rudi's toe, and was about to hook my ankle, all without Mr Augustus noticing a thing–he was far too busy chatting up Miss Patsy through the staffroom window.

I could feel Celeste getting closer and closer behind me. My heart was beating so fast I didn't know which one would escape first–my legs from her stick or my heart from my chest, but my efforts were futile. There was no way I could outrun her.

It was as if she blamed me for our team scoring against hers, even though I wasn't anywhere near Beau when she scored the equalising goal. I'd been hovering several paces behind, as usual.

*WHOOSH!*

There it went again. Another strong gust of wind, this time blowing twigs from the willow trees and a couple of broken pinecones straight onto the pitch. Most of us managed to dodge the spikey foliage but Celeste was too busy stalking my ankles, and the ball, so she didn't see a large pinecone on its side in the grass. She tripped right over it and fell heavily to the ground losing her hockey stick in the process.

Beau quickly passed the ball to Emi, who passed the ball to Rudi, who passed the ball to Suki, who passed the ball to me. I froze. I had never had my teammates pass me the ball before. I was always too busy fretting over my own ankles, so scoring an actual goal had never occurred to me, and now the team were counting on me to not let them down.

"Shoot, Fleur, shoot!" Suki yelled. "You can do it!"

Yes, I could.

I would.

Fleur Marie Bottom could do this.

*WHACK!*

My right ankle was on fire. Pain shot through my bones forcing me to collapse on the grass like a newly felled tree. I don't know how she did it, but Celeste had somehow recovered from her pinecone calamity and reached my ankles before I even touched the ball.

My ears went all muffled, and the pain was excruciating as I struggled to regain composure. I looked up at the sky and could've sworn I saw Nan's green slipper. Then her lavender cardigan seemed to flap ferociously above my head. Was I suffering from concussion?

Distant sounds slowly became clearer as I recognised cheers

from the yellows (mainly Celeste), who had scored a second goal for her team in the last sixty seconds of the match.

The final whistle blew.

"2-1 to the yellows," Mr Augustus said. "Well done, everyone. Don't worry, reds, that was a great effort, and we've still got another two practices to enjoy before the deciding match on Friday. It's your last day of Primary School too, so let's make it one to remember. Then one of you lucky teams will be playing for the Farrow Park Cup during the summer holidays!"

"Enjoy?" muttered a voice somewhere close to me. "Who's he kidding? They were terrible, weren't they?"

I peered around to see who was talking but could only spot two mischievous squirrels, perched on a skinny branch of a crab-apple tree. Whoever had said it was right. I was terrible! Beau and Lydia helped me up. I vigorously shook my head in the hopes that it might take away some of my ankle pain.

"We've got you, Fleur. Are you okay?" Lydia asked.

I nodded.

"You've got to say something, Fleur. This has gone on long enough. You won't have any ankles left at this rate," Beau whispered.

"It's okay, it's not that bad," I said. "Don't say anything. Please. You know she'll only start on you or one of the others if you do."

What was wrong with me? Why couldn't I stand up to Celeste and tell her that the way she treated people, the way she treated me, was unkind and wrong? Beau nervously bit her bottom lip as Mr Augustus came bounding over.

"Doing okay, Fleur?" he asked, concerned.

Beau and Lydia raised their eyebrows hopefully.

"You two go on ahead with the others. I'll be there in a few minutes," I said to them. They nodded and caught up with the reds to walk back to class.

The yellows had already skipped off the pitch to a chorus of 'whoops', 'yesses', and 'get-ins', although Celeste had strangely held back. She hovered near me, folding bibs into equipment bags.

"Fleur? Anything you want to tell me?" Mr Augustus asked. This was it. This was my moment to come clean and tell him all the horrible things Celeste had said or done since she'd arrived at our school. My chest tightened at the opportunity to finally shift the heavy weight of worry that I had been carrying around with me for months.

"Well, it's Celeste," I muttered. "She keeps tripping me up on purpose and doing other mean things too."

There! I had finally plucked up the courage to be honest. My chest felt lighter at once. Perhaps I should have confessed sooner.

"What do you mean, tripping you up? I didn't see anything. Did Leena put you up to this?"

"What? No, of course not." I said, horrified.

"Look, I know she was cross that I took her out of the match to recover, but it's not your place to get involved. You'll have seen matches on the telly where other players interfere with a ref's decision, and it never ends well, does it?"

"No, you don't understand. It's not just that; there are other things too–"

Mr Augustus raised a hand to stop me talking. "Come on, Fleur. I'm not about to give you a yellow card so don't worry. You're wanting to stick up for your friend, and that's admirable, but let's play by the rules, shall we? Cut Celeste a bit of slack. It's not nice to have people gang up on you, telling tales. Plus, she's still new, and desperate to fit in, and we want to make her feel welcome, don't we?"

Celeste grinned behind Mr Augustus's back, making an 'L' shape with her finger and thumb, silently calling me a loser.

"That settles it then. Let's get back to class."

Celeste quickly ran ahead to catch the others before Mr Augustus caught her. He trudged along too with bags full of equipment. I stayed where I was and fizzed at being told off for telling the truth. How could Mr Augustus have got things so wrong? He was useless!

*WHOOSH!*

A swirl of cold air blew a scent toward me that smelled strangely familiar like rose petals and peppermints. It reminded me of Nan.

I looked down to check if the bruise on my ankle had surfaced yet, as last week's injuries went black straight away. There was zero evidence of anything so far, but a chess piece slumped in the grass diverted my attention. It was a black rook with hand-carved bricks, climbing ivy, and a castle door etched into the soft wood. Upon closer inspection, it looked exactly like the one from our chess set at home. Wait a minute, it *was* the one from our chess set at home.

Further along the pitch where the grass met the tarmac playground, I spotted something else. A scuffed and shabby, reddy-orangey notebook lay face down, almost as if it had been dropped from a great height. There was no mistaking it–it was Nan's book but what on earth was it doing here?

# CHAPTER EIGHT

## *The Book*

The walk home from school took me slightly longer than usual, thanks to a throbbing ankle and bruised pride. I waited until I was alone before I found a free bench near the pond in Farrow Park, I needed space to read Nan's book. It was nice to be momentarily free from the burden of Celeste and Ruby and Anais–even though I knew it would be tomorrow soon enough. At least the ducks appeared fearless. They glided along the water's surface, making gentle ripples with their silky wings, and gathered in front of me.

"I haven't got any bread, you know!" I jibed.

Ducks might look graceful, but I don't trust them anymore than any other type of bird. Not after they joined in with the mass mobbing of my head the other week.

There were eight ducks in total. The largest one scuttled in front of the smaller ones and steered them sharply away from me. I wasn't wearing a onesie made of barbed wire! I might not like them, but I wouldn't hurt them. The lead duck looked on with indignation as he floated past.

"We actually prefer peas, pea-brain! Don't you know

anything?" he said, before whizzing further across the pond.

I gasped loudly. I saw that duck move his beak and talk to me, and this time there was no denying it.

I stood, scrutinising the area around me to make sure nobody was watching. These voices were becoming too much of a coincidence now. Part of me didn't want to believe it was true, but I couldn't keep ignoring it.

Yes, this was all totally, mind-blowingly petrifying, but on the other hand, how incredibly cool! My excitement got the better of me because by the time I had thought of something else to say to the stroppy duck to test out my talking abilities, they had disappeared behind an island in the middle of the pond.

I finally reached inside my school cardigan and unclenched my armpit, which is where I had kept Nan's book since the end of hockey. I didn't want to risk anyone getting hold of it or reading it before me. Celeste had been watching me like a hawk all afternoon, like she could sense something was out of place, although I was pretty confident that she hadn't suspected a thing.

I had to find out what was so important to Nan that meant she never strayed far without it. I did one final sweep around the park to make sure I was alone–apart from the ducks bobbing back into view occasionally–the coast was clear. I quickly opened the first page, which read:

*If found, please return to:*
*Nellie Prudence Bottom*
*673 West Everitt Road*
*North Fincham*

*London*
*NNE1 0ZE*

I didn't know Nan's middle name was Prudence! It made her sound ancient. I know she's old at nearly ninety, but she doesn't act it. Not with me anyway.

I turned the page to the first double-spread, hoping to find something revealing. My tummy flipped at the thought of what Nan might have written. Something that might be of assistance to me, for example, 'What to do if you suddenly find out you can talk to, and understand, an African Grey parrot, and possibly a shed-load of other animals.' That kind of thing.

I couldn't believe my eyes when I read:

*Crackers*
*Peppermints*
*Prawn Cocktail Crisps*

It was Nan's shopping list! I sighed, there must be something in her book worth reading. I looked through the first few pages and there was nothing exciting to see at all. It was just full of shopping lists and addresses.

I skipped ahead a few more pages which, disappointingly, included more of the same. List after list, more addresses, worst shops to buy wool.

Nan's book was fast turning into a bore-fest. Until I reached three pages from the middle and things started to get interesting.

*10:52am: Elsie Steaddington arrives home.*

*11:15am: Stanley Burrows leaves Klassy Kutz.*

*12:20pm: Raymond Anderson catches the number 32 bus (double-decker).*

Row upon row of timed entries stared me in the face. They went on and on, page after page. I flicked further forward: two, four, eight, twelve pages and it was all similar stuff. Line upon line of recorded movements of people I didn't know, apart from Elsie Steaddington who has lived around here since, well, forever. Why would Nan be spying on other people she barely knew?

I tried searching for clues elsewhere in her book and eventually, six pages from the back, I found a page entitled 'Special Gifts'. It didn't look like your average list of birthday present ideas. For a start, Nan had included herself at the top. Something didn't add up as I forensically examined every word that followed:

***Special Gifts***

***Nell Bottom:*** *Invisible Flyer and Gift Spotter (Aerolator and Spylator)*

***Elsie Steaddington:*** *Unknown*

***Stanley Burrows:*** *Sticky Hands (Gripalator)*

***Raymond Anderson:*** *Magnetic Skin (Magnalator)*

***Evan Quayle:*** *Disappears (Disalator)*

***Sol Durston:*** *Speed (Boltalator)*

***Fleur Marie Bottom:*** *Talks to Animals? (Animalator)*

I dropped Nan's book in shock. It landed in a dried-up puddle, which covered my feet in dust. There was too much to take in. Was any of it true? Flying? Magnetic skin? Nan?! Why would she have written that stuff down? It was baffling. Unthinkable.

Suddenly, Nan's age struck me. I felt terrible for thinking it, but what if she was losing her marbles? I mean, come on, there was no way she could fly. It was ridiculous. Nobody could fly. Not properly. Not unless you were a movie star supported by a million special effects. Besides, if one of my family members announced they could fly, I was pretty sure I'd have known about it beforehand. You couldn't live that close to someone without knowing, could you?

I was left with only two possibilities for Nan's silly book entries: age-related dementia or a lively imagination. As her mind was still sharper than mine and Mum's put together, I settled on the second option.

I restlessly tapped the bench and jiggled my feet, because, what if there was an option three that should've been option one in the first place? That Nan might actually have written the truth all along because it sure had looked like her slipper and cardigan in the sky this morning. And I definitely could hear Sir Barclay and some other animals talking. I took a deep breath. What if magic was an actual thing and I really was an Animalator?

I picked up Nan's book and held it against my chest. Nan

had a lot of explaining to do. I closed my eyes towards the sun trying to process it all, but there was so much to take in. Nan, Sir Barclay, animals, magic. Where did it begin? Had Nan known all this forever? It upset me to think that she had kept humongous secrets from me. Why didn't she tell me? She could trust me. I wouldn't say a word. Not if she didn't want me to.

Startled by loud quacks, I spotted the same group of ducks coming back towards me. It felt like as good a time as ever.

"Excuse me!" I said to the lead duck who still looked cranky. "I know I can hear you and I think you can hear me, but can you understand everything I say?"

The duck said nothing.

Aaagh! What was I thinking? I should've stuck with option two and a lively imagination. Perhaps *I* was the one losing my marbles.

"Got any peas yet, lady?" the duck suddenly asked.

No way! He could hear me! My tummy bounced excitedly. "Sorry, I don't."

"In that case then, no. I'm afraid I can't understand a word you're saying!" And with that, the line of ducks disappeared a second time. I suppose I deserved that.

An eerie flutter echoed behind me in the trees making me feel uneasy, but I couldn't see anything. It was just me, on my own, staring into the same egg-stenchy pond.

"*Squawk!* Don't you know that you should never take something that doesn't belong to you? *Squawk!*"

I didn't need to open my eyes to know that Sir Barclay was perched on a branch right above my head.

# CHAPTER NINE

## *Dizzy Spell*

"What are you doing here?"

Sir Barclay had now flown down to perch next to me, his sharp claws wrapped tightly around the wooden bench.

"It's a free country, isn't it? *Squawk!*"

I supposed it was, but I had never been this close to Sir Barclay before–ever. For a grey, obnoxious, feather-bum, he was rather striking in the sunshine. The ruffles around his neck were soft and smart, and his jet-black beak looked like Nan had spent the whole day polishing it. I hoped she used one of her clean hankies.

"Is it true?" I asked, closing Nan's book tight.

"*Squawk!* Is what true? I haven't the faintest idea what you're talking about."

Okay, I got it. He was playing hard to get. Not wanting to reveal to me how much he did or didn't know, and I couldn't blame him. But it didn't make his ludicrous game of cat and mouse any less frustrating.

"About Nan!" I said. "Can she really invisibly fly?"

I bit the inside of my lower lip until it hurt. I did want

to find out what was going on and how much of it was real, but part of me was also scared that I wouldn't like the answer.

"*Squawk!* No," he said. "She most certainly does not invisibly fly."

"Oh."

Her book really was just full of boring old Nan lists and facts then? That shot down my silly flying theory, didn't it? Although, it still didn't explain how Nan's book *and* the hand-carved chess piece made their way from the sky on to the school field, but perhaps there was a logical explanation I just hadn't found yet.

My tummy relaxed. It was probably for the best that I didn't have an invisibly flying Nan, it just made all the entries in her book even harder to understand.

"As I said, she doesn't invisibly fly. *Squawk!* She invisibly blusters!"

"What do you mean?"

"*Squawk!* I'm afraid her technique isn't as refined as it used to be, and then there's her hips. Her flying reactions are not as fast anymore either. I've tried warning her, Fleur, but she never listens."

I jumped off the bench. "So, she can invisibly fly? It was her on the hockey pitch today, wasn't it?"

I had so many questions that the thought of being able to speak with Sir Barclay suddenly felt less frustrating and more beneficial.

"How on earth should I know?" he replied. "I'm not her keeper. She is as free to roam the skies as I am. *Squawk!*"

Something wasn't right. Nan was obsessed with Sir Barclay.

Mum even once suggested that he was Nan's most treasured possession after Grandpa Willie died because, in a way, he helped her to feel less sad and lonely. He brightened up her days.

"She didn't tell you what she was planning to do today?" I asked. "She didn't tell her prized parrot that she intended to secretly fly over her granddaughter's hockey practice?"

"*Squawk!* Of course, she did. She's been on about following you to school for ages. She suspects something is, how do you say? Awry. *Squawk!*"

"A-what?"

"Awry," he replied in an exasperated tone. "All not being well. Not as it should be. If you must know, she's worried about you, but I told her not to be. *Squawk!* I said if you had concerns at school that you would be smart enough to talk to her or your mother."

My heart sank. If only Sir Barclay knew that I'm not in the slightest bit smart. That I haven't properly told anybody how mean Celeste is because they'll probably think I'm telling tales, just like Mr Augustus did. Plus, I keep hoping it won't last and that she'll soon get bored.

"She didn't listen to you then?" I asked.

Sir Barclay's pupils darted from side to side. His feathers more ruffled. Less smart. "*Squawk!* Not exactly."

"What do you mean?" I asked. "What's going on?"

He twitched his pupils and dipped his neck. "Oh, very well, then! If you must know, your nan did say she was going to fly over your hockey match to see if you were alright and yes, I told her not to because of her old age and failing health, but the problem is. . ."

"What, Sir Barclay? Come on, spit it out!"

"She can't hear me! Alright! She never has and I doubt very much that she ever will."

He side-clawed away from me until he was perched at the very end of the bench.

"Oh," I said, surprised. "I thought Nan must be able to talk to you too."

Clearly, I had got things wrong. I was sure I'd overheard Nan talking to Sir Barclay, about the weather or if she should have another cup of tea, and he always replied. I guess Nan simply hadn't understood what he'd said.

"Sadly not, Fleur. I wish that she could, but she only hears my squawks."

Sir Barclay turned his little grey face away from me like I sometimes do if I'm about to cry and I don't want anyone to see me.

He sighed. "*Squawk!* We have an understanding that's more powerful than words. She talks and I listen. I know everything about her, what she thinks, what she'd like to do, what she wishes she had done. I know all her secrets, which she trusts me with because she knows I will never tell, because I can't. *Squawk!* We have a strong bond, you see, that means we look after each other in our own way. Does any of this make sense to you?"

I nodded. It really did. More than Sir Barclay realised.

"*Squawk!* Don't get me wrong," he continued. "I try to give her the odd hint so we can communicate. I'll fetch her a pen if her old one runs out; move her glasses before she sits on them; switch the kettle on if she complains about being parched. *Squawk!* I help her with the little things and in return she helps me. She doesn't know how she's helping me, obviously, but all the nosy neighbouring she does with her telescope and jotting everything down in her book, helps me immensely, or at least I hope it will, one day."

Suddenly, I felt a strong sense of pride in this super-stuck-up African Grey parrot who could have upped and left Nan anytime he liked. Anytime the window opened, and the fresh scent of freedom lured him out, but he didn't. He stayed in the attic-room with Nan, and always returned to his Birdrobe to be by her side.

But I couldn't ignore the burning question I'd had since he first mentioned Nan's book yesterday. "What is it you're looking for, Sir Barclay?"

"Ahh," he exhaled, his eyes brighter and happier than I had ever seen them. "I'm searching for my one true love."

"What? Pineapple cheese and crackers?" I joked. I couldn't help it.

"You see! This is why I am less than thrilled to find out *you* can hear me, and not somebody more sensible. *Squawk!*"

I didn't mean to laugh. I knew better than anyone how it felt when someone made fun of you. Celeste did it to me every day.

"I'm sorry," I said. "I didn't mean to be silly, please–what's your one true love?"

He glared at me. "Not what Fleur, but who. To find a human being who can hear and understand me, means I'm one step closer to finding my one true love again. My dear Jenny Jen. The warmest, kind-hearted, most fun-loving, and beautiful African Grey lady parrot you could ever wish to meet. My wife, Fleur."

Wowsers Trousers! Sir Barclay had a wife? I didn't see that one coming!

"So where is Jenny Jen now?" I asked carefully.

"She's not Jenny Jen to you! She's Dame Genevieve Monroe Ophelia Smythe!"

I covered up my giggle straight away. Sir Barclay rolled his eyes. I knew the pompous fluffball was still hiding amongst his vulnerability somewhere, but I forgave him for it. Plus, I liked the name Dame Genevieve Monroe Ophelia Smythe. It sounded regal.

"That's the problem. I have no idea where she is. I need someone who can understand me to help find her. I need an Animalator. Honestly, Fleur, you've no idea how special you are."

No, I didn't, and my head was starting to ache with it all.

Sir Barclay was getting more upset as he flapped and paced along the bench. "*Squawk!* We were flying back to England after a break in Italy last year. You see we've always lived separately in different houses, with different families because, we've found that people are more accepting of parrots if indeed, there is only one. Everyone assumes we're noisy, but that's not the case for us African Greys–it's those garish Macaws who give all birds a bad name. *Squawk!* Anyway, Dame Genevieve loves the sunshine on her feathers, so we stayed an extra day to enjoy the landmarks of Rome. Fascinating place. Only we were in the middle of the Colosseum, when–"

I gasped. "Did she die?"

"No! She did not! *Squawk!* At least I hope she didn't. We got separated in a freak rainstorm that started in Italy and followed us all the way home to England. Now, I don't know where she is." Sir Barclay's little face dropped.

"Is she still there?" I whispered, not wanting to cause him more sadness.

"That's my greatest fear, Fleur. I left without her!"

I'd never had the urge to hug a bird until now. "Don't worry. We'll figure it out. We'll find her together. I'll help any way I can."

"*Squawk!* Do you really mean that? You'd do that for me?"

Actually, no, was my honest answer. I wasn't doing this for him. I still didn't trust him, not fully. He was still sitting on at least eight of my missing chess pieces, I was sure of it, but I'd do it for Nan because I know how much she loves him.

"Of course, I'll help," I replied. "Come on, let's head home now. We can tell Nan about it together."

I started packing Nan's book and the hand-carved rook into my rucksack.

"*Squawk!* We can't do that! You mustn't. Please don't tell her about Dame Genevieve, Fleur, or that you can hear me. It'll change everything between us."

"Change things how?" I frowned. Surely Nan would be only too happy to help Sir Barclay find his wife? And I could always translate their conversations for them.

"How would you feel if all your private thoughts suddenly became public? *Squawk!* Or everything you said when you were alone was being secretly recorded?"

"Well, I suppose I'd feel a bit angry, betrayed maybe."

"*Squawk!* Exactly! And that's why I want to keep this from your nan. I don't want to hurt her. I don't want her thinking that I've used our friendship for my own gain, because I haven't, Fleur. We've both helped each other out. *Squawk!*"

His small frame was motionless. No swooping, no twitching, no flapping. No nothing.

"Can't we keep this between the two of us, for the time being at least? Please Fleur."

I didn't like keeping something this big from Nan. I mean, I knew she'd been hiding bigger things from me, but she must have had her reasons. In the same way that I'd held on to Celeste bullying me because it was embarrassing to admit that I was being bullied. Mr Augustus thought I was telling tales, so why would anyone else believe me? Besides, I'd not wanted to worry Mum or Nan with it all because of everything that happened with Dad and Grandpa Willie. They were both still coming to terms with not having them around anymore and they didn't need anything else to worry about.

I tickled the mole on my cheek, and Sir Barclay inched closer to me, which unnerved me even more. He was the one who'd first made me realise I could hear animals, so maybe if I helped him, he'd help me understand it all. The magic, the Animalation and more importantly, Nan's book.

"Okay, Sir Barclay."

"*Squawk!* Thank you, Fleur."

We sat together on the bench looking out across the murky pond, strangely enjoying the peace and quiet after an exhausting day.

"Fleur! Fleur! Is that you?"

I leapt up and knocked my open bag onto the floor.

Mum was dashing across Farrow Park clutching her handbag and wearing her 'I work in an antique shop outfit', which today included a pair of beige, cropped chinos, blue, spotted T-shirt, and an odd-looking necklace made from shells and pasta tubes.

"Hurry up, love, we need to go."

"Over here, Mum." I waved. "Are you okay? What's the matter?"

Mum ran around the pond and put her hand on my arm.

"We need to go, love, it's your nan. She's had a dizzy spell."

# CHAPTER TEN

## *Believe Me*

The smell of bleach and plastic hit the back of my throat harder than Mum's grip around my body. She was hugging me so tightly that I was worried she might break a bone. We were huddled in a poky, mint-green hospital room with Nan hooked up to a million wires and machines. We didn't know what was going on, or if Nan would be okay, and the thought of her not being okay made me sick with fear.

Mum eventually loosened her arms and blew her nose loudly. The two nurses checking on Nan, jumped, and turned around as though they half expected to see a herd of elephants stomping through the ward.

"Sorry!" Mum whispered as she carefully wiped the tears from her eyes without smudging her mascara. "It's just dreadful. I can't take it in. One minute, I'm saying goodbye to her as she's tucking into a bowl of porridge, and the next she's in here, struggling to breathe."

"Try not to worry, Mrs Bottom," the plumper of the two nurses said. "Her heartrate has settled and we're running some further tests to see what's the matter with your mother-in-law."

"Big Bottom!" Mum replied.

"I beg your pardon?" the nurse said curtly, as she smoothed the creases of her uniform over her waist.

"Oh gosh, I'm sorry! I didn't mean *your* big bottom! I don't think you've got a big bottom at all, it's a lovely bottom—as far as bottoms go. What I meant was, that's what my husband and I used to call Nell. Big Bottom. Well, before he left us because she's the older Bottom in our family. It's a little joke we shared between us."

Why did Mum always have to make such a fuss about bottoms? As if having Bottom as our surname wasn't bad enough, she always had a knack of making things even more embarrassing than they needed to be.

"Hmmm." The nurse didn't look convinced. "The doctor will be in to have a word shortly so make yourselves comfortable. There's a water machine in the corner and a coffee shop down the corridor." She wrote something on Nan's clipboard, rubbed her hands with pink gel, and walked out.

"Right, yes, of course. A comfortable Bottom is a happy Bottom. Isn't that right, Fleur?"

I nodded because rolling my eyes felt too hurtful under the circumstances. The nurse had barely left the room when Mum started to sniffle all over again.

"It's okay, Mum," I said. "Try not to worry."

Nan had to be fine. She just had to be. I didn't know what we would do without her.

"Phftphftphft!" Mum blew her nose again. "Sorry, love, it's just the shock. I'm all over the place. I think I need a strong cup of coffee to sort me out. Do you want to come with me to the shop? Choose a juice or something?"

"I'm good, you go. I'll stay here," I said. "In case Nan wakes up."

She would wake up–wouldn't she? She had to. How could I deal with all this stuff without her?

I pulled the chair closer to Nan's bed. She looked older without her glasses on, less sparkly. It was a wonder anyone could sleep with the different machines beeping and humming around her ears. Her little chest moved slowly up and down like a bird. Thank goodness she was still with us.

Tap. Tap. Tap.

I looked at the machines to figure out where the noise was coming from, but it wasn't them.

Tap. Tap. Tap.

The doorway was clear; nobody was outside or waiting to come in.

Tap. Tap. Tap.

I looked across the room and saw a concerned, feathered face staring back at me from outside the window. Sir Barclay!

"Oof!" I muttered, as I heaved the window open a crack. There was no way Sir Barclay could squeeze his way in. His head was far too big for a start. "Sorry, Sir Barclay, this is as far as I can open it."

"*Squawk!* That's cheap architecture for you. Typical! Always cutting corners." Sir Barclay dipped his head up and down to see Nan through the streaky glass. "How is she? *Squawk!* Do they know when she'll wake up?"

"No, not yet. But I'm sure it'll be soon. "

"*Squawk!* Your nan is one of the toughest humans I know. She's just not always one of the smartest. Honestly, flying around at her age in the midday heat, making mischief on a hockey pitch. *Squawk!* She won't have drunk enough water."

My heart ached because Sir Barclay was right, and I knew it was all my fault. If only I'd had the guts to tell Nan or Mum about Celeste, then maybe Nan wouldn't have flown over the school to check on me. She'd be back at home, safe in her green armchair, wearing her un-matching green and purple slippers, ready to beat me at chess.

"Fleur, is that you?" Nan's voice was softer than normal as she struggled to get her words out from underneath the transparent oxygen mask covering her face and helping her to breathe.

"Nan! It's me! Are you okay?" I raced across from Sir Barclay and stood next to her bed, clasping her frail hand in mine.

"You've nothing to be sorry for, baby, but you must listen to me."

"*Squawk!* She's awake!" Sir Barclay erupted. "*Squawk!* She's awake! Don't just sit there, Fleur! *Squawk!* Tell someone!"

Sir Barclay's flapping made such a fuss it was a wonder he hadn't disturbed the dead. It was lucky Nan couldn't understand what he was saying although the squawks would still be deafening.

"Shh," I said. "Just give us a minute, will you? Nan's trying to tell me something."

"Did you say something?" Nan asked. "I didn't quite catch you. It's all these tubes. Either that or your mum's right about my hearing after all." She let out a little chortle, which quickly turned into a chesty cough.

Sir Barclay continued to flap furiously until he changed

tack, repeatedly pecking on the window instead to make his point fully known.

"*Squawk!* Hurry up, Fleur! Go and get a nurse or a doctor! *Squawk!*"

"I will, just give us a minute!" He was beginning to wind me up now.

"Fleur?" Nan frowned. "Who are you talking to? Listen to me, baby."

"Sorry Nan."

Her fragile eyelids bobbed up and down. They were paper-thin, like butterfly wings.

Sir Barclay was now strutting along the window-ledge, pecking the window and thin air. Could he have been any more annoying? I got the message!

"Shall I nip out, Nan, and get Mum or one of the nurses? I won't be long."

I stood up, but Nan tightly clutched my hand, making me wince.

"Fleur, baby, wait. This is serious."

So was keeping Sir Barclay quiet but I couldn't tell Nan that. I felt as though I was fizzing, as panic filled my entire body. Was Nan about to share her dying wishes with me? I didn't know what to do. I glanced at the window and saw the irate parrot flapping, strutting and squawking outside.

"I'm not going to cark it yet, if that's why you're looking so worried," Nan said reassuringly, which helped to reduce the fizzy feeling. "But I'm exhausted so you need to listen to me. Quickly, before your mum gets here and puts me on a three-bean bouyon diet."

I couldn't help but laugh. I glanced at the window. Sir

Barclay had finally disappeared too, so I could at least give Nan my full attention. I sat on the bed, and Nan held my hand even tighter than her hair bun, which appeared to have loosened against the stiff pillows. Nan pulled off her face mask and knocked it to the floor. It was the first time I noticed three, spiky whiskers growing out of her chin. Really long ones.

"Secrets are exciting, Fleur," Nan said, her eyes repeatedly flickering open and shut. "But the minute they make you feel worried and uneasy, that's when you realise they're not actually secrets anymore–they're problems, and believe me, problems don't disappear–not until you've dealt with them properly."

I tried to swallow the boulder-sized lump in my throat, because I immediately thought of Celeste and how she treated me. Was this Nan's way of warning me that she knew about it? Or that I had read her book? That I knew about magic? She suddenly opened her eyes fully and placed her bony hand on my face. It was freezing cold.

"Promise me that you won't bottle things up, Fleur. Can you do that for me? It'll only make things worse in the end." She tapped my temple gently with the tip of her finger. It was like ice. "I'm talking about what's in here. Don't ignore what's going on. Because your true gifts will–"

SMACK!

Sir Barclay faceplanted the window, making me jump up in fright. He was annoyingly persistent.

"*Squawk!* What are you two jibber-jabbering about?" Sir Barclay didn't appear to have hurt himself as he continued to grow more furious and more flap-some outside Nan's window. "Fleur Marie Bottom don't ignore me! *Squawk!* Tell me what's going on!"

Two sparrows and an overweight pigeon flew down onto the same ledge.

"Can't you keep the noise down?" one of the sparrows asked. "You're giving us a headache!"

"Sounds like there's a party going on outside that we're not invited to." Nan smiled. "Such a lovely sound, though, isn't it? The chirping of birds." She closed her eyes.

I couldn't think straight with Sir Barclay tapping and flapping outside along with the other disgruntled hospital birds. Nan was trying to tell me something important. I sprang up from the bed and yanked the window shut to hear Nan properly, silencing Sir Barclay in the process.

"Sorry, Nan. What were you saying?"

"I said, don't ignore what's going on in your mind because your true gifts will only shine through when you face your biggest fears. Bottling up your worries won't do anyone any favours; believe me, I know all too well what happens when–"

"Nell!" Mum squealed, sloshing hot coffee all over the mint-green floor. "Oh, thank goodness, we thought we'd lost you!"

Nan remained silent, unable to finish what she was trying to tell me, as Mum was already covering her face with kisses before calling the doctors and nurses to join us.

Nan opened her eyes again. They were still full of sparkle and glistened away.

"I'm not going anywhere just yet, my dear–believe me."

# CHAPTER ELEVEN

## *Zimmer Somersault*

It was strange sitting in Nan's bedroom without her, especially in the dark. We had reluctantly left her in hospital overnight on doctors' orders–something about final checks and observations.

Mum had been asleep on the sofa for almost an hour since we got back. I decided not to wake her, opting instead to tiptoe up to Nan's attic-room and read the rest of her book. It was still in my bag, along with her chess piece, both of which I would put back where they belonged before Nan twigged they were missing. I also wanted to see if Sir Barclay needed anything.

He wasn't there, but the window was wide open for his return. The balmy scent of takeaway pizza and exhaust fumes wafted around Nan's room as I peered out to see if he was nearby. He wasn't, but I stayed anyway to watch life going on around me because Nan had the best view of the street from her little window.

You could see the hustle and bustle from the shops. Cars to-ing and fro-ing along the main road and in contrast, the tranquillity of Farrow Park opposite. I liked watching it unfold. I felt involved yet hassle free, which was a million miles from how I felt on a hockey pitch.

As I sat on the window seat, which was scattered with bright yellow, white, and blue patchwork cushions, it occurred to me that this could be the spot where Nan watched everyone below and wrote all the timed entries in her book.

"Ow!" I said as I wriggled to get comfy.

Something hard poked into my hip from underneath the cushions. I dug about to see what it was and pulled out two items. First there was a pen that had bite marks around the red lid, followed by a weird telescope thing. Bingo! This *was* the spot where Nan did her spying.

The smooth, metal telescope felt cool in my warm palm as I inspected it. I already knew Nan had ridiculously strong hands after she squeezed mine at the hospital. The weight of the telescope confirmed it fully because mine quickly started to ache. It didn't look very startling. It was short and chunky, like an old piece of pipe, and the only distinctive feature was a raised button halfway down the middle. I pressed it firmly, and the short telescope quickly grew to the size of a flute. I moved it close to my eye and peered through the lens. I couldn't believe it! I could see for miles. Naughty Nan! This wasn't some shoddy piece of kit, this was a serious telescope used by a serious spy, perhaps even to undertake a secret mission.

Its reach was incredible. I could literally see the tiny teeth of a tabby cat chomping on a discarded kebab up the road. The seemingly black tiles on the roof of St. Joseph's church, which were in fact green, thanks to an eruption of ivy and moss around its chimney. The white 'smalls' hanging from Mrs Ball's washing line and (according to Nan's supersonic lens) turned out to be a pink floral pattern and not so small after all.

I moved Nan's powerful telescope to the right of Farrow Park and towards the row of terraced houses across the street which looked exactly like ours. My gaze immediately glued to Elsie Steaddington who was creeping through Farrow Park using her three-wheeled walking frame for extra support. It was called a Zimmer Ultraweight Plus. I wouldn't have spotted it in a million years without the telescope.

Elsie was wearing a poppy-red, knitted dress and yellow cardigan, which had two buttons missing from the bottom. According to Mum, Elsie Steaddington has always lived around here since Mum was a little girl at least, and she is famously known by everyone for being incredibly S. . . L. . . O. . . W.

I mean, it was great that she got out and about so much at her age, but it was bad luck if you got stuck behind her on the walk home from school. Even the snails overtook her! I watched her painfully make the trip through Farrow Park towards her house, all scrunched and hunched over her Zimmer frame, taking care with every step, pausing frequently to catch her breath. To you or me, she was about thirty seconds away from her front door. At Elsie Steaddington speed however, she was at least another twenty minutes off.

Then something strange happened which made me sit bolt upright. Instead of walking out of Farrow Park and along the busy road to her front door, she paused against the row of tall conker trees behind her back garden. She edged herself a little closer–checking first that nobody else was around and then–*PING!*

Elsie Steaddington sprang from her knees, into the air, and somersaulted over the large trees. Not once, not twice, but THREE TIMES! Still clutching her Zimmer frame. I couldn't believe it! The slow, old lady who was even smaller and frailer than Nan, had mounted a twenty-five-foot tree and landed neatly in her own back garden on the opposite side of her fence.

Nan was right! She knew Elsie Steaddington had a special gift; she just hadn't fathomed out what it was yet, but I had. I bit the skin around my fingernail to distract me from missing Nan and the amazement of what I had witnessed. It didn't feel right though. Nan should've been here with me. She should've been the one witnessing Elsie's amazing twenty-five-foot tree somersault, not me. This was all becoming too much, but what should I do now? What would Nan do?

I nervously clicked the bottom of Nan's pen, replaying in my head what Nan had said to me at the hospital. "*Believe me, my dear.*"

Of all the things she could have said to me, why did she choose that? What was so important that she wanted to tell me in secret and out of everyone else's range? There had to be more to it.

I racked my brain trying to recall our whole conversation, missing out the bits where Sir Barclay had acted like a spoilt, squawking loon. I knew he wanted to make sure Nan was okay, but she hadn't asked to talk to him first, had she? She had wanted to talk to me.

It was upsetting to flash back to Nan's hospital room seeing her looking old and weak. It brought back all the sadness that had happened over the last year, like losing Grandpa Willie, and saying goodbye to Dad. I put my hands over my face and rubbed my eyes. Yes, things could've turned out differently, but they hadn't, and I was beyond grateful that we still had Nan. I slapped my cheeks to snap me out of my lull and get back to remembering what Nan had said before she was smothered by Mum's coffee-breath kisses.

That was it. She had started telling me not to bottle things up. About not ignoring my feelings so that my true gifts could shine through. True gifts! That was it! I jumped down from the window seat and found my schoolbag, where I had safely left the chess piece and Nan's book earlier. It was obvious. I didn't know why I hadn't thought of it before. Nan would write down what she had seen using her special gifts–whether that be invisibly flying or telescope detective work–in her book. I knew what I had to do for her. I had to write down exactly what had just happened like all the other stuff she had captured.

I fumbled around in my schoolbag desperately trying to find Nan's book, which I was sure I had put back. My frustration quickly turned to tears as I realised Nan's book and the chess piece were nowhere to be seen. I must have dropped them earlier.

In desperation I looked through Nan's telescope to see if Sir Barclay was around. He could help me. He was the only one who could, but disappointingly, he was nowhere to be seen. I scoured the sky, the lampposts, the tiled roofs, but nothing. He had completely disappeared.

I zoomed the lens to the bench where Sir Barclay and I

had sat before Mum told us about Nan, and my whole body grew hot. Hotter and sweatier than Nan's stuffy hospital ward, because I knew exactly what had happened to Nan's book.

I watched a girl bend down to pick something up from underneath the bench. She stood, glancing around furtively, clutching Nan's chess piece and notebook. I recognised the smirk instantly. Of all the people to find Nan's missing things, why did it have to be Celeste?

I crunched my teeth together fiercely. I didn't know who I was most cross with–Celeste for finding Nan's book, or me for dropping it in such a hurry. What if she had already uncovered Nan's strange entries in the middle and put two and two together? It might've sounded like a stretch too far, but it wasn't entirely impossible.

This was a disaster, and for the first time, I wished I had opened up to Nan and told her everything that had been going on at school recently. If I had, then she would be snuggled up in her armchair right now instead of lying in a horrible hospital bed.

I followed Celeste with Nan's telescope as she dashed back to the main path then stopped abruptly. Up ahead, Ruby and Anais were energetically waving to get her attention. She quickly hid Nan's book behind her back, then stuffed it down into her waistband, and pulled her T-shirt over the top, obscuring it from view. The three of them then waltzed off without a care in the world, and all I could do was watch.

From Nan's bedroom, I continued to hunt high and low along our street. Celeste, Ruby and Anais had disappeared, and to make matters worse, I still couldn't find Sir Barclay anywhere. The only observation of mild interest was next door's cocker spaniel, Freddie, jumping up and down at his gate. I whistled down to the wagging ball of excitement to see if he could hear me. What was I thinking? Of course, he would hear me. It was a whistle, and he was a dog.

But then, I thought, what if he could actually hear me? As in, hear and understand me talking to him, like the other creatures and animals I had heard the last couple of days. I still thought the idea of me being an Animalator was staggering, but my heart also fluttered crazily, because as staggering as it was, I knew it could happen.

"Freddie! Freddie!" I called out. Freddie looked up, confused, unsure where the high-pitched voice had come from. "Up here, Freddie! There's a good boy!"

He clocked me the second time around and seemed to get even more excited although he didn't talk back. This was unusual. Did this mean not all animals could hear me after all? I rubbed my forehead and contemplated my next move. I decided to give it one more try.

"Freddie! Hi, Freddie! You haven't seen our pet parrot lately, have you? Small, feathered thing with a big attitude!" Sir Barclay would be most disgruntled with the 'pet' reference, but he wasn't around to comment.

Freddie jumped up and down again, his tongue flapping in the evening breeze. "Afraid not." He panted. "Sorry, I've only just been let out." I bent my knees and clapped. It had worked! I had done it! It still felt bonkers, and it was going to take a long time to get used to being an Animalator, but that's what I was. Now I needed to find Sir Barclay, fast, to help me figure out what to do next.

# CHAPTER TWELVE

## *For Nan*

"*Squawk!* Heads up, nosey!" Sir Barclay swooped in through the window. His sharp talons narrowly missed my eye and Nan's telescope.

"Sir Barclay, thank goodness! Where have you been? I was worried about you; you've been gone ages." I sniffed. Relief at seeing him and knowing animals could properly understand me had turned me into an emotional wreck. "Oh, Sir Barclay. I've got tons to tell you, please, you've got to help me. I'm in such a mess."

"*Squawk!* Oh, now you want my help! *Squawk!* Shame you didn't think of this at the hospital earlier when you shut me out!"

"Look, I'm really sorry about that, but Nan was trying to tell me something important."

He wasn't interested and had already settled his claws on the middle perch in the Birdrobe that Nan had made for him. "*Squawk!* Poppycock! There's nothing more important than your nan's health, Fleur. You were just being selfish. Wanting to keep her all to yourself. *Squawk!*"

"What?! No, I wasn't. I was trying to do what she asked only you kept twittering on! She only wanted a minute with me," I protested. "And she was fine. They've said she'll make a full recovery and might even be home by Sunday."

Sir Barclay pointed his pompous beak towards the ceiling and pretended not to hear me, but the way he flinched his head to clear his eardrums was a dead giveaway. I could tell he'd heard me perfectly.

His rudeness was starting to irritate me like it had the night we first spoke when Nan nipped downstairs to the toilet. I clenched my fists and could feel my neck growing hot. Why had he been so insistent on stopping Nan from talking to me at the hospital? We had literally just agreed to work together as a team to figure out a book, wife, and chess piece plan.

"Aren't you pleased?" I asked. He twitched his head once more and continued to ignore me. "Given you were so worried about Nan and her health, I thought you might be a little more relieved." Finally, he looked at me. "Why were you so persistent at the hospital? Are you sure it was only Nan you were concerned about?"

"*Squawk!* And what's that supposed to mean?"

"Oh, I don't know." My neck felt hotter than ever. "Maybe you were more worried I was going to tell Nan about us and Dame Genevieve."

"What? No! Certainly not!"

Boom! I had caught him out.

"Oh, come on, Sir Barclay! If you really care for Nan as much as you say you do, then now's the time to be honest."

"Oh, alright! I admit it. *Squawk!* I'm sorry, Fleur! I was worried that you'd tell her everything and that she'd feel betrayed, because where would that leave me? If it's not your secret hospital chats, it's your cosy little chess games where I get ignored in the corner, watching the pair of you have all the fun. It's not like you genuinely need me, is it? You could quite easily ask your nan or any other animal to help you figure out your special gift."

He sighed and dropped his shoulders. Why hadn't I noticed it before? Sir Barclay was jealous of what Nan and I had together!

"Yes, I could, if I really wanted to, but I haven't, have I? Because I don't want to. I'm pretty sure that if Nan knew we were having this conversation, she'd want us to stick together and help each other out."

Sir Barclay nodded. "I'm sorry, Fleur. *Squawk!* I suppose I just hadn't expected your nan to discover you as an Animalator."

"That makes two of us then." I laughed. "Look, why don't we agree that she loves us both and that we both love her too? You and I vying for her attention or bickering about who she loves the most isn't going to help her get better, is it?"

My dalliance with African Grey parrot negotiation seemed to be going better than expected. I finally felt as though I was getting through to him because old fluff-pants was inching closer to me—without looking as though he wanted to peck me.

"We'll get her back soon," I added.

"*Squawk!* Only when she is sufficiently strong, rested, and recovered, Fleur and not a moment sooner. *Squawk!*"

"I wasn't just talking about Nan."

He raised his feathery brow and gave me an inquisitive glare that made my neck go all prickly because I was worried I had overstepped the mark.

"I'm talking about Dame Genevieve Monroe Ophelia Smythe too," I explained. "She's definitely out there somewhere, and we'll find her soon, I'm sure of it."

If I didn't know any better, I'd say that Sir Barclay had softened. I could almost make out the faint crack of a smile beneath his beak. Either that or he had wind.

He bowed his head in agreement. "*Squawk!* That's kind of you to say." He flapped over to where Nan kept her kettle. "What else have you got your plaits in such a twist for anyway? The hospital hasn't phoned, have they?"

I clenched my tummy muscles hard to stop the tears from flowing.

"No, Nan's fine." I said, looking down. A small tear dropped onto the floor and I quickly wiped it away with my foot. "But I've lost her chess piece!"

"*Squawk!* That's nothing new! She's always losing her chess pieces. One more won't make a difference."

I quickly checked his expression. His guard was down, and I knew he was responsible for pinching the missing chess pieces, even though I still hadn't found them. He even said it himself–he was jealous of how Nan and I enjoyed our chess games together.

"This one's different. It's one of the really special ones from the set that Grandpa Willie made," I wailed. "And it gets worse. I've lost Nan's book too!" I covered my eyes with my hands. There was no way I wanted to let Sir Barclay see me cry.

"Are you sure? *Squawk!* I thought you had it? Right before your mum told us about your nan's dizzy spell."

Sir Barclay flew over and landed on my shoulder,

encouraging me to calm down. I gasped, until I saw his eyes, and then I realised he was only concerned. We gazed at each other in Nan's mirror in front of us.

"I did! But I accidentally dropped it without knowing. Oh, I've made such a mess of everything. Nan's poorly because of me, you've lost your wife, I've lost my friends, and now I've lost Nan's book and chess piece too! I'm useless!"

"*Squawk!* You're not useless, Fleur. You're just trying to deal with things on your own, which is tough for anyone, let alone a ten-year-old. How on earth do you expect to manage life's difficulties if you insist on keeping everything to yourself?" Sir Barclay shifted over to the end of Nan's bed.

"What should I do?" I asked.

"You mean, what should *we* do? *Squawk!*"

"You'll help me find Nan's book?" I asked doubtfully. "And chess piece?"

He nodded.

"Then we'll tell Nan about Dame Genevieve? No more secrets, once and for all?"

He hesitated, his beady eyes pulsing as he mulled over my question. "*Squawk!* Oh, alright then, yes, Fleur. We'll do it all together, for your nan."

"Good." I smiled, feeling the tension in my face melt away.

"*Squawk!* But if we're telling your nan about Dame Genevieve, you've got to promise you'll tell her your secrets too." I paused for thought. "About Celeste."

I knew what he meant. It was a fair enough request, but I didn't like the idea of it. It was embarrassing to admit that I was being bullied, and what if Nan didn't believe me? Or, like Mr Augustus, she thought that things weren't as bad as

I was making out? I twiddled my plaits in silence as I chewed Sir Barclay's suggestion over further. He did appear to be on my side, didn't he? And I supposed I would have to tell someone eventually.

"Alright then, fine." I said eventually. "When the time's right."

Sir Barclay bowed his head again, almost gratefully, as I agreed to his suggested terms.

"Don't look so worried, Fleur. Your nan's not that scary! She'll think of a way to help you out."

"That's not what's worrying me. I mean... well... of course I'm worried, but there's something else."

"*Squawk!* Go on," Sir Barclay said tentatively.

"Celeste's got them both," I blurted. "I saw her pick them up after I'd seen Elsie Steaddington somersault over a twenty-five-foot conker tree."

"*Squawk!* Hang on a minute! What? When? How can you be so sure?"

"I used that thing." I pointed at Nan's telescope, which I had slung on to Nan's bedcovers earlier.

"Well, well, well!" Sir Barclay chuckled. "Looks like your nan might have some serious competition on her hands! Let's get our beaks together pronto and hatch a plan to stop that horrible bully causing you further misery. *Squawk!*"

Nobody could replace Nan. She was one of a kind. The most magical Bottom ever. But Sir Barclay was right. I had to get her book back from Celeste, and quick, before anyone else found out the truth about our special gifts.

# CHAPTER THIRTEEN

## *Mustard Cardigan*

I helped Mum make up the sofa bed in the living room ready for Nan's return from hospital on Sunday evening. I felt like I had run the length and breadth of twenty hockey pitches the amount of times Mum had me running up and down the stairs, but it was worth it to make Nan comfortable. Nan wasn't enthralled about the idea of sleeping downstairs, but Mum was insistent, and after much moaning and groaning, she finally agreed.

I barely got a chance to say hello when Mum walked her in, let alone catch up on matters of magic and missing books. Mum didn't want Nan disturbed, so I spent the whole evening plumping cushions, fetching hankies, and making endless cups of tea.

"Come and see me in the morning," Nan whispered as I gave her a goodnight hug.

Only our early-bird plan was thwarted by Mum who was on guard before I had even walked down to the kitchen. All we managed was a quick goodbye and an air-blown kiss before Mum ushered me out of the door in the direction of school.

"Settle down please, everyone. We've got a busy last week ahead of us, so let's get going," Mr Augustus said.

He had suspiciously swapped his usual mustard cardigan and matching tie, for a non-condiment-based navy tracksuit. It wasn't that I had anything against navy, but a tracksuit only signalled one thing: hockey practice.

"Come on, everyone, pay attention," Mr Augustus bellowed over the noise of our classroom chatter.

Ugh. I didn't like the sound of this.

"Instead of our usual morning schedule this week, as we're almost at the end of the school year, we're going to spend thirty minutes each day practising sports, so we're fully prepared for our matches on Friday."

Why did he have to remind us about Friday when I had a morning's worth of ankle smashing to get through first?

"Remember, whoever wins their Friday matches will represent the school in football and hockey for the Farrow Park Cup in August. It's an amazing opportunity!"

I rolled my eyes. No, it wasn't. It was an opportunity to get a broken foot.

"Hurry up, boys! Get your football kits on, go, go, go!"

The boys didn't need any further persuasion and had already scurried towards the PE bags hanging from the hooks in the corridor.

"You too, girls. Get yourselves ready for a quick bash about on the bottom field."

A quick bash about? What was he trying to do? Send my

already quivering nerves into overdrive? It had worked. This was the WORST Monday of my life.

As the boys laughed and enjoyed their football practice on the opposite side of the field, our hockey pitch was a tale of two halves. At one end, Celeste and the yellows cheered eagerly. At our end, you could hear a pin drop as we all waited anxiously for the whistle to blow.

"Up front, Anais! Quickly!"

It didn't take long for Celeste's toe-curling shriek to occupy the air. Anais dutifully ran ahead to receive Celeste's pass.

*WHACK!*

I jerked around, expecting to see somebody hurt, but it turned out to be Celeste who had successfully knocked the ball to Anais. Once Anais had escaped our pitiful line of defence, she tapped it back to Celeste who slammed it into the back of the net.

"Goal!" Celeste grinned and high-fived her elated teammates.

We were only minutes into the match and the yellows had already scored. If this was how practice was going to be, Friday would be torture.

Leena, sporting a rigid frown, propelled herself towards the ball, which had been re-released back into the centre of the pitch. After a scuffle with Clara on Celeste's team, and some fancy footwork between her and Jade, Leena somehow managed to reach the goal line.

"Goal! Right back atcha," Leena jeered. She seemed to be the only person in our team, in our entire school, who was prepared to stand up to Celeste.

Celeste glared back in response.

Mr Augustus blew his whistle as the sun beat down upon us. How I wished for a holiday. Preferably with Mum and Nan to St. Lucia, far away from hockey and Celeste.

"Lovely team passes, girls. Well done, keep it up!"

Celeste ignored Mr Augustus's encouragement and got straight back to work.

A recognisable silhouette flew directly above me and rested on a nearby birch tree.

"*Squawk*!"

What was Sir Barclay doing here? I thought he wanted to stay at home and settle Nan back into her room.

"*Squawk!*" Sir Barclay hovered above me and a couple of other girls. What was he up to?

*WHOOSH!*

He circled closer, hovering inches above our heads. Everyone saw him and exchanged worried looks, except Mr Augustus who was too busy chatting.

"What are you doing?" I whispered. His face was blank. Why couldn't he hear me?

*SPLAT!*

The dirty rascal pooed all over Leena's face! She was covered in sticky, white goo. It was in her mouth, up her nose, and right across her eyes. She couldn't see a thing!

"Aaagh!" Leena squealed, flapping her hands in disgust.

Celeste chuckled and made a rapid dart for the ball. She scurried it away from Leena who continued to shriek uncontrollably at being covered in African Grey parrot poo.

*SPLAT!*

He did it again! Everyone looked on, horrified, as Beau was struck next. Celeste howled, loving the distraction Sir Barclay was causing. She seized the ball, glued her eyes to Sir Barclay's flight path, and somehow dodged his bottom missiles.

*SPLAT!*

Another shot blasted out of his bum and landed on Azari. It was revolting! I couldn't just stand and watch everyone get showered with Sir Barclay poo. I had to do something, unlike Mr Augustus, who had turned his back on us to investigate something by the bike sheds with the caretaker.

"Oi!" I muttered crossly under my breath.

Beau and Leena glanced over and pointed at themselves, confused. I panicked that they might have seen me talking to Sir Barclay, so I quickly deployed 'Operation Distraction', otherwise known as a big, fat, lie. "Oi. . . err. . . you two. . . are you okay?"

"No, Fleur! We're not! Look at us!"

Phew. They hadn't noticed. Too busy comparing the thickness of their face sludge.

"Oi!" I repeated. This time whispering, "What are you doing? Stop it now. You're helping the wrong team! If you're desperate for a poo, then aim towards Celeste, not us!"

The pompous old bird completely ignored me and proceeded to attack Suki, Tiggy, Jasmine and Emi, as the yellows raced ahead, clean, and oblivious. I thought we had sorted out the whole hospital window thing. He couldn't still be mad at me. We had a deal, didn't we? I was going to help him find Dame Genevieve and he was going to help me get Nan's book and chess piece back from Celeste. Why the sudden backtrack?

Two squirrels jumped onto a lower branch as if not wanting to miss any action.

"I think you're going to need a cloth, aren't you?" snorted the smallest of the two.

"You think?" I replied sarcastically, throwing my hands in the air. "Is there any way you could stop him? He's not listening to me!"

"Nah, no chance. Bigger than us, 'aint he? An' how could we stop him without wings?"

He had a point, and it was a silly question to ask, but I didn't know what else to do.

My tummy flipped as I noticed that Celeste had caught me interacting with the squirrels. She turned her eyes back towards Sir Barclay instead. If she had any sense, she'd avoid him at all costs.

*SPLAT!*

I had taken my eyes away from Sir Barclay for a nanosecond, choosing the squirrels over African Grey bird spotting, and now I had sloppy, parrot poo on my face. It trickled down my cheeks and onto my neck. Ugh! It was still warm. I wiped my eyes with the sleeve of my T-shirt, and saw Celeste proudly air punch, and give Sir Barclay a humongous thumbs-up. A sickly feeling swirled around my insides. Sir Barclay knew how I felt about Celeste. How she constantly bullied me. Why had he turned against me?

*WHACK!*

"Ow! You did that on purpose!" A familiar thud suggested another player had collapsed. One of our reds I bet, no doubt injured by the smiling Celeste assassin.

"And goal!" Celeste cheered.

Mr Augustus finally stopped chatting to the caretaker and blew his whistle loudly.

"That's it, girls. 2-1 to the yellows. Well done every–yikes!"

Mr Augustus gritted his teeth in revulsion at the scene in front of him. Faces, arms, and shoulders covered in poo, alongside red players who had cowered under nearby trees.

"Good grief! What happened? I only took my eyes away for a minute."

"We weren't happily playing! We were screaming to escape parrot poo!" Beau said.

"A parrot? That shouldn't be outside. Where is it now?"

Sir Barclay landed on top of a monkey puzzle tree behind us looking extremely smug. His red tailfeathers dangled down to reveal three white spots on the ends of each feather that I hadn't noticed before.

"Mr Augustus, that's so unfair!" Leena screamed, edging towards him. "That stupid bird totally sabotaged our chances of winning!"

Mr Augustus backed away, putting some distance between him and Leena's crusty face. "I agree it definitely shouldn't be flying about outside," he said. "And it has made a bit of a nuisance of itself, hasn't it? But. . ."

But what? He couldn't possibly be siding with Sir Barclay now too. I wanted to grab his wig and shove it in the bin, but I didn't want the poo travelling further down my arms.

"But they're fascinating creatures, aren't they?" he continued. "I believe they originate from Africa, and their pooing antics are an instinctive reaction to predatory pursuit."

Was he for real? We weren't the predators! Sir Barclay was! Mr Augustus seemed more concerned about Sir Barclay's welfare than ours. Charming!

"Does anyone know who it might belong to?" he asked.

My mouth shrivelled as I felt the flaky poo drying around my nose. Sir Barclay had nothing to do with me. Not anymore. Everyone covered in poo shook their heads tetchily. The smirking yellows shrugged, silently delirious with their win and clean faces.

"The game should've been automatically stopped, Mr Augustus," Leena said, still fizzing with rage. "There's no way the yellows should've won!"

"Don't worry, Leena, we've got time to clean up before class. A wet paper towel, some hand sanitiser, and a bit of vigorous scrubbing will soon shift the stuff."

Who was he kidding? This wasn't a bit of bird poo on our faces, we were covered in sloppy, parroty, bird poop. We looked like yetis.

"Calm down, everyone. You can try your luck again in the morning. It's just a game. It's all about taking part and having fun."

Oh, I was glad he mentioned the 'fun' part, I'd almost missed it!

The yellows swaggered back to the classroom, patting Celeste on the back. I swear she walked slowly on purpose to rub her victory in.

Without warning, Sir Barclay ferociously beak-bombed from the monkey puzzle like a fighter jet. Splat, after splat, after splat. The remaining reds and I ducked in true domino style, one after another, in fear of parrot poo reprisal.

"Aaagh!" Mr Augustus screamed, dropping his clipboard, and frantically waving his arms. "Get it away from me! Get it away from me!"

Sir Barclay made one final 'deposit' on top of Mr Augustus's wig. Both Celeste and I stopped in our tracks to watch Sir Barclay's next move. Everyone else covered their heads and ran back to the classroom, but before I joined the others, I spotted Celeste ping up her thumbs again, so I waited. Sir Barclay squawked, nodded, then flew off in the opposite direction. I was stunned. Had they been in cahoots with each other the whole time?

"That's it!" Mr Augustus yelled. "The field is out of bounds until I've had a chance to conduct a thorough risk assessment."

"What about our hair and clothes?" I asked, still reeling from the stench of poo and Sir Barclay betrayal. "My T-shirt's ruined. There's no way this stuff will come off using paper towels." I brushed my cheek. It reminded me of sandpaper.

"Right, of course," he replied, suddenly full of concern. "Try a large splodge of soap onto a warm, wet, paper towel first. That should do the trick. If there isn't a suitable top in the lost property box, then you can borrow one of my cardigans."

Great. This wasn't just the worst Monday ever; this was the worst day of my life. And all because of that scrunched up, dirty-bottomed parrot. There was no point being able to talk to animals. This gift wasn't special at all. It was worthless. Just like every word that had come out of Sir Barclay's beak, and I knew I had been right all along. I HATED birds.

# CHAPTER FOURTEEN

## *Spotty Tailfeathers*

I had already decided that rocks were too hard. Sticks were a bit pointless–he wasn't a dog–and shoes were rather limiting. Unless you could put lots of different types of shoes into a bag and fire them like rounds of ammunition. Cushions, on the other hand, would do the job perfectly. Feather cushions to be precise, as they're plump and heavy, and don't make a noise when they land on the floor. Bonus.

I could casually walk up to Nan's attic-room, pretend to peer out of her Velux window, then *WALLOP*. I'd fire patchwork cushion, after cushion, after cushion, towards the treacherous fluffball, and give him a dose of his own medicine for covering me and the rest of our hockey team in his revolting poo.

I burst through the front door, eager to get hold of Nan's cushions, and quickly dumped my bag in the hallway. The strap had rubbed against my neck, which was already sore from being scrubbed with paper towels earlier. I spotted a note from Mum stuck to the end of the banister, informing me she had taken Nan out for a drive to the chemist to pick up a prescription. Good. I could deploy my cushion hurling plan immediately and without being told off.

Upstairs, I launched one of Nan's window seat cushions towards Sir Barclay who, up until that point, had been enjoying a late afternoon rest in a sunbeam.

*WALLOP!*

He shot out of his feathers just in the nick of time. Drat.

"*Squawk!* What in the name of. . . Fleur Marie! What are you doing? *Squawk!*"

*WALLOP!*

I launched the second cushion, even harder this time, yet somehow, I still missed. If I'm honest, I always thought Sir Barclay was a little overweight, which I put down to all the cheese and biscuits he scoffs, but as it turns out, his heavy frame is actually quite light. He's basically all feathers and beak, which was bad news for me, as he was proving to be more agile and difficult to clout than I expected.

"*Squawk!* She's gone mad! Somebody call the police! *Squawk!* Or the army! *Squawk!* Or my mummy! In fact, scrap that, call Fleur's mummy. Cindy! Where are you? Your daughter appears to have lost her mind!"

He flapped over to the window, knowing full well that I couldn't hurl anything else at him for fear it might land on some poor soul loitering underneath, or worse still, Mrs Naylor's prized flowerpot.

"Do you know what, Sir Barclay? Squawk away! Nobody's coming to rescue you. It's just you and me."

The upset of the day had grabbed hold of me like a boa constrictor, squeezing its body tight around my throat and preventing me from wriggling away.

Sir Barclay looked aghast.

"I knew I could never in a million years trust you, but I tried, honestly I did, for Nan. Like we agreed. Only you turned your back on our agreement, didn't you? For Celeste! And why? Because you're jealous of Nan playing chess with me instead of you! Ridiculous! Is that why you keep pinching our chess pieces too?" I shrieked. "Or is the real reason you keep taking them because your bird brain is so small, that you can't actually play?"

It was immediately clear I had ruffled Sir Barclay Wigbert Titus Smythe's royal feathers as he snapped his head forward in repulsion.

"*Squawk!* How dare you!" he replied. "I have nothing but the greatest respect for your nan. *Squawk!* Something, which indeed *you* could benefit from learning."

"Respect? Oh, that's a good one coming from someone who poos his way out of his problems!"

I heard a long, sharp, sucking noise that sounded a bit like a whistle. Only it wasn't. Sir Barclay had inhaled the longest breath ever recorded and almost turned purple.

"I BEG YOUR PARDON?" he squawked. "I have never. *Squawk!* Nor will I, ever, poo my way out of anything! What do you think I am? Some kind of animal?"

I might only be ten years old, but we had recently learned about rhetorical questions in school, and this felt like it might be one, so I decided to keep quiet for a minute.

Silence.

And then another minute.

And then one more.

And then a final one for luck.

"Alright then," I said, "how many other scrunched-up African Grey feather-bags are there 'coincidentally' lurking about in the school playground that you know of? Conveniently ready to aim, and fire, a bum-full of pineapple cheese and crackers at us while we're trying to beat Celeste and her terrible team at hockey?"

Sir Barclay's feet wobbled on the ledge of the Velux window as he leaned further in. Now I had his full attention.

"You mean, somebody actually pooed on you during your practice match? On purpose?"

"Duh!" I said, tapping the side of my plait before I extended my arms to display the full horror of Mr Augustus's spare mustard top.

Why was he pretending to be clueless? It wasn't every day I came home with flaky bits of bird poo stuck to my ears. It didn't make any sense.

"*Squawk!* But that's preposterous!" he said. "Why would anyone do such a thing?" He flew to his Birdrobe and rested on the top perch.

This animal was becoming more infuriating by the second. If I knew the answer to that, would I be standing in front of his wrinkled face, wasting my breath?

"Do you think," he began, after a few seconds of pondering. "What I mean is, could it be in any shape or form as a result of you wearing that dreadful top? What colour is it anyway?"

It was an undeniably horrendous colour, but it was either accept Mr Augustus's cotton mix top or stay in my own foul T-shirt. I didn't fancy prolonging the stares and giggles from everyone who had become fascinated with my bird poo encrusted face, neck, and hair, so I reluctantly changed. I spent my entire lunchbreak trying to scrub it off my skin and it still wouldn't budge. It was like concrete.

"It's mustard, if you must know, and I didn't exactly have much choice in the matter. I can't get this stuff off. Seriously, what did you eat?"

"I keep telling you, Fleur, it wasn't me. Do you really think I'd betray you, your nan, and our plan, over a silly squabble through a hospital window? I thought we'd moved on from that. *Squawk!*"

"So did I! But maybe Celeste came up with a fancier plan that you couldn't ignore!"

"I've never spoken to Celeste! Honestly, Fleur, you're not making any sense."

I sighed. I was already exhausted from the poo-fest, and the shouting had begun to make my head bang too. I knew what I had seen. Sir Barclay and Celeste were communicating with each other, I just hadn't figured out why.

"Well, if it wasn't you, then who was it?"

Sir Barclay dipped his head up and down whilst simultaneously side-clawing along his perch. "*Squawk!* I don't know," he eventually replied. "Are you sure it wasn't a pigeon? They really are the vilest creatures especially with their toilet habits. We've all tried telling them not to keep eating crumbs off the ground, but they never listen. *Squawk!*"

I tried to scratch a lump of white bird poo off my elbow, but it wasn't shifting.

"It wasn't a pigeon, Sir Barclay. It was an African Grey parrot with a face like yours." He immediately made the horrible, breath-sucking whistle noise again. "Okay, what

I meant was, it looked like it had a face like yours." He loosened his body.

"*Squawk!* Just because we're all grey, doesn't make us all identical you know. We each have our own special features. Not quite the same as your special gifts, but special to us, nevertheless."

My special gift didn't feel very special today, but I knew what he meant. I didn't feel like I was any closer to getting an explanation from him either.

"So, what's your special feature then?" I asked, keen to pursue other 'it might not have been Sir Barclay who pooed on us all' scenarios. He twitched his beak.

"*Squawk!* If you must know, it's my eyes. To the normal, unappreciative human, they are purely black and white. *Squawk!* But if you look closer, you can see that mine have faint swirls of red within my pupils."

I crept closer to him, half expecting him to fly off. I wasn't going to throw any more cushions at him, but he didn't know that which is why he followed my movements across the room with extra suspicion.

"Can you see?" he asked, as I stood directly in front of him.

I could. They were beautiful. A small vortex of colour swirled in each eye.

"I thought you were going to say your spotty tailfeathers," I replied. "I hadn't noticed them properly until today, and they're quite something too, aren't they?"

Sir Barclay frowned. "*Squawk!* I don't have spots on my tailfeathers. *Squawk!*"

I stood back and peered at his bottom. His feathers had a

thin red stripe along the ends and not a white spot in sight. This was weird. Something was wrong.

"No, it's not possible. *Squawk!* It couldn't be. . . could it? *Squawk!*"

"What couldn't it be?" Now he was the one not making any sense. Something was afoot because he was pacing like he did at the bench before Nan's dizzy spell.

"I don't have any special spots on my tail feathers. *Squawk!* But someone special to me does."

It smacked me in the face like projectile parrot poo. It was so obvious.

"Your wife!" I shouted. "Dame Genevieve Monroe Ophelia Smythe!"

"*Squawk!* Exactly, Fleur! She's alive! *Squawk!* She's alive!" He repeatedly nodded his head in excitement. "She must've been petrified of you all. *Squawk!* It's an instinctive reaction, you see, all the pooing. It's basically a sign of distress. My poor Jenny Jen. Fleur, we've got to find her."

I held off with the clapping and congratulatory cheers for a moment, preferring instead to tap my chin with one of my plaits. It was perhaps fair enough that Dame Genevieve didn't engage with my pitch-side conversation, but she had engaged with Celeste. There had to be more to it.

"I'm not sure, Sir Barclay. She didn't look petrified to me. She looked in control, and it certainly felt targeted towards our red team. Why else would the yellows get away poo-free?"

"CELESTE!" we both shrieked.

"If she's as mean as you say she is, then she must have put Jenny Jen up to it. She must be keeping her somewhere! At her house perhaps? *Squawk!* Hurry up, let's go. Because if we find Celeste, we might find Dame Genevieve and your nan's book at the same time. *Squawk!*"

Yes, he was right. This was much more plausible than Sir Barclay turning rogue and doing a runner with Celeste. I felt guilty for even thinking it and tried to forget my mistake by jogging on the spot, and playfully kicking Nan's cushions to celebrate.

Sir Barclay flapped excitedly and flew around Nan's room performing somersaults. I stopped playing cushion-football and caught my breath.

"There's one thing we've missed," I said now, standing still and being serious.

"What's that? *Squawk!*"

"If Celeste did give Dame Genevieve orders, then surely..."

"Surely what? *Squawk!*"

"Surely she must be an Animalator too."

The penny had dropped, along with our faces.

The door creaked open as Sir Barclay and I gazed at each other, both numb and surrounded by Nan's beach-themed, patchwork cushions, which lay strewn across the bedroom floor. Nan leaned against the wall, holding onto the door handle for extra balance.

"Who must be an Animalator?" she asked, clutching a white paper bag.

# CHAPTER FIFTEEN

## *Shoddy Shed*

There was only one thing more annoying than Mum's burnt cooking, and that was the fact that she wouldn't leave Nan alone. Nan had barely placed one un-matching slippered foot in her own room, when Mum dashed up the stairs behind her, destroying any chance of a magic-related chat.

It was lovely having Nan back in the attic again. It felt normal and cosy. At least it did once I picked up Nan's cushions. . . apart from Mum's constant presence. I helped Nan into her armchair under Mum's watchful eye, and she playfully thumped down, lifting both feet hidden inside one green and one purple slipper. Nan and I had a lot to catch up on, but it would have to wait until Mum left us alone.

"Has anyone seen my notebook?" Nan slid her hand down each side of her chair.

I gulped and looked at Sir Barclay, who discreetly switched the kettle on with his claw, while Mum laid out Nan's bedclothes.

"No," I said innocently. I pushed the squashy footstool right up to Nan's chair and sat directly opposite.

"I'll have a look downstairs later," Mum said, turning her back on us to straighten Nan's pillows. "I might've taken it down by accident when I tidied up earlier."

I puffed out, relieved knowing Mum's comment was a complete stroke of luck, and that she wouldn't find it anywhere. I couldn't take my eyes off Nan's un-matching slippers, further evidence that recent news reports about flying arms, legs, and slippers, were somehow linked to Nan.

Nan's eyes twinkled as she caught me examining her slippers. "Everything all right, baby?" She covered one side of her mouth with her hand and whispered to me while Mum's back was turned, "Have you got something you'd like to ask me? Or are you just going to sit there staring at my feet all day?" She raised her eyebrows then popped a peppermint in her mouth from a little round tin stuffed in her cardigan pocket.

"I'm fine," I said. I smiled when I realised Mum was looking our way while folding Nan's clothes. "Now you're up here where you belong. I don't know what I would've done if you hadn't come home."

Mum suddenly burst into tears. "Agreed!" She stopped folding and pulled us together for a hug. "Now look what you've done! I'm a blubbering wreck! Let's put some music on quickly to cheer us all up." She walked over to Nan's radio, switched it on, and jiggled her hips while she continued sorting Nan's nighties.

Nan nodded along. "Don't fill your mind with 'what ifs'. They only distract you from what's here."

Nan always worried about my mind. Maybe it was time I gave it some care.

"What were you trying to tell me at the hospital the other day?" I whispered.

Nan checked that Mum was occupied, crunched her mint and swallowed. "I'm glad you asked, because–"

"Right, Fleur Marie!" Mum said above the music. "Your nan's had quite enough excitement for one day. Come and do your homework downstairs. You can keep me company while I cook tea."

"But Nan's fine! Aren't you? We were just about to play a relaxing game of chess, weren't we?"

I made sure to use all the right words associated with rest and recovery, but Mum was adamant Nan needed peace so there was little point in me arguing.

"It's fine, baby," Nan said holding up her palm to calm the mood. "Do as your mum says. All the excitement of choosing pills at the chemist has tired me out." Nan smiled as I stood, and Mum walked towards the door. "Yes, a nice relaxing half-hour up here watching the world go by," Nan continued, holding my gaze tight. "It's not like I can fly about and cause any mischief, is it?" She winked at me knowingly as Mum chortled at Nan's suggestion.

Only Nan wasn't kidding, and she knew I understood her hidden joke. Nan held out her arms for a hug and gently pulled me in.

"Your mum will mellow soon, baby, don't worry. She's got a kind heart and only wants to look after us," she whispered as she gave me the biggest cuddle.

"I know," I said, melting into her body. "I missed you, Nan."

"I missed you more," she replied, planting a whiskery kiss

on my cheek. "We'll talk properly soon I promise, and in the meantime, you've always got Sir Barclay!"

My heart pounded but I didn't pull away. I reciprocated with a kiss on her cheek, which smelled of a cross between antiseptic cream, aniseed rock, and toothpaste. Mum coughed impatiently from the door, and Nan patted me on the back–gentle reassurance that confirmed she knew I was an Animalator.

I waited until Mum's favourite antiques programme was in full swing before I spoke to Sir Barclay again as it felt too risky with her hovering around.

"Where are you going?" Mum asked as I shuffled off the sofa.

"I'm going to Ruby's for a bit, if that's alright?"

"Ah that's nice. Course I don't mind. Back before teatime though."

"Got it," I said, already heading up to my room for my jumper.

"*Squawk!* You took your time, didn't you?"

Sir Barclay had flapped down from Nan's room and was currently perched on my bedroom windowsill, which he had never done before today.

"What are we going to do now?" I asked. "Start looking for Dame Genevieve before she disappears again?"

"*Squawk!* I've already flown uptown, over the school, and Farrow Park, and it's all clear. She could be anywhere. How can we even be sure Celeste has her? *Squawk!*"

I flushed with anger. "She's got her. I don't know how

or where, but that horrible little twerp has managed to get everything that belongs to us."

"*Squawk!* I know you're upset, but you're not unkind. Try not to let her get to you."

This time I flushed with embarrassment. It wasn't easy being kind to someone so mean.

"Maybe I could pinch her schoolbag tomorrow? See if she's left Nan's chess piece or book in there," I suggested hopefully. "There might even be a clue about Dame Genevieve."

"*Squawk!* I don't want you getting into trouble by looking into other people's bags. No, let's do as you first suggested and start with Celeste. Come on, if we're quick, we can fly over to her house now and see what she's up to. No time like the present. *Squawk!* Think about it, Fleur, it's the only way to protect your nan and prevent the truth about her gifts and your gifts from being revealed. *Squawk!*"

Sir Barclay saw me chew the string of my hoodie. The thought of snooping around Celeste's house and coming face-to-face with her terrified me more than hockey practice.

"*Squawk!* Don't worry, Fleur, you're not alone. You've got me. Come on!"

My hands felt cold and jittery, and I didn't like the sound of it one bit, but I knew there wasn't another option.

I only knew where Celeste lived because I had heard everyone at school bleating on about how it was the biggest house on Station Road. I hadn't been there myself, which made standing in front of the enormous white house with three double garages even more daunting.

"Told you it wouldn't take us long," Sir Barclay squawked from a lamppost.

"Speak for yourself," I panted, trying to recover from the uphill struggle from Farrow Park to Station Road. "It might only be ten minutes from home but it's not easy when you don't have wings!"

I checked my watch: 4:43pm. Mum's show, *Tat and That*, would finish soon, and then she would start cooking tea. We had to hurry.

Celeste's house was incredible. She had more windows on one side of her house than all the sixty-eight double-decker buses that passed our house each day. And then there were the cars. All sparkly clean, and proudly parked on the gravel drive in a horseshoe shape. Imagine having enough cars to make a horseshoe shape! Mum struggled to keep our Vauxhall Corsa on the road, so how anyone could afford four vehicles was beyond me.

Sir Barclay swooped down in front of the number 30 glass plaque on the wall near Celeste's grey front door.

*CLICK. CLICK.*

Two sets of security lights shone onto the driveway, lighting up Celeste's house and hanging baskets even more than the late-afternoon summer sun. Clever Sir Barclay! He had done that on purpose to give us a better idea of where to avoid being caught.

The door opened and a grey cat shot into the porch. Celeste's mum bent down and stroked its head before pulling down her purple-rimmed glasses to take a better look outside. Her spiky, silvery hair glistened as she peered left and right.

"Meow! Forget the outside! It's getting too cold, feed me instead! Meow!"

Unimpressed by the lack of attention, the cat poked its ears backwards before swishing its tail grumpily and heading further indoors. After a few seconds of checking the drive, Celeste's Mum was met with none other than the ankle-bashing, hockey-thrashing bully herself.

"What is it, Mum?" Celeste placed her hand on her mum's shoulder, eager to peer out over the top of it.

"Nothing, darling, go and finish your homework. Probably just a bird or a cat or something."

"A bird? What type of bird? Not a grey one with spots?" Celeste asked, craning her neck to peer further out.

Her mum blocked the exit with her arm and dropped her plush, lilac scarf on the floor. "What? No! A brown one, I think. It will have flown too close to the security sensors again. Why the sudden interest? You haven't done anything silly again, have you? This is your last chance, remember?"

Last chance at what?

"Can I go out and play before tea? Please? Five minutes, then I'll come straight back in, I promise."

"No, not tonight. I've got some work I need to do in the basement and besides, you've only got a few days left at school before we fly out on our next adventure. Lockton High School is expecting big things from you, and so am I. Head down, less hockey, and no trouble. It's time you acted like a proper Hexter. One to be proud of."

Lockton High School? Sounded like a prison to me, but the thought of Celeste not joining me at Shepson High School was brilliant news! I clicked my fingers excitedly. At last, I would be free from her meanness! What did her mum mean by a Hexter? The door slammed before I had time to think. As soon as they had gone inside, Sir Barclay ushered me around the side of the house.

"This way, Fleur! *Squawk*! Follow me."

"I keep telling you, I can't go as fast as you! Where are we going anyway?"

After Sir Barclay circled the perimeter of Celeste's house, sticking his beak on almost every window, he turned his attention to the row of conifer trees at the bottom of Celeste's garden. Behind them was a rickety wooden greenhouse–which was growing more damp and fungus than actual vegetables–and a shoddy garden shed.

The shed windows were blacked out with thick tape, and a new padlock protruded from its door. Sir Barclay perched on top of the moss-ridden greenhouse opposite and watched as I investigated.

"*Squawk!* I can't see anything of interest around here."

"Shh! Can you hear that?"

He flapped over to my shoulder and we both pressed an ear to the door.

A radio was on. Why would anyone be playing music in an empty shed?

"*Squawk!* Never mind songs, we're here to find your nan's things. Let's try somewhere else before we run out of time. The treehouse? Garage? *Squawk!*"

"Hang on a minute!" I said, craning my neck with one eye closed. I focussed on the tiny sliver of window that hadn't been properly taped up. "I can see something."

"Come along, Fleur! *Squawk!* We've got to get going!"

"But I can see. . . there's the radio. . . and a light."

"I don't want to attend a disco, Fleur. Honestly! *Squawk!*"

Sir Barclay flew onto the greenhouse roof unimpressed.

"Wait a minute, I can see a cage, Sir Barclay!" My breath frosted up a mouth-shaped section of window. Sir Barclay flapped closer. "There's something red and spotty! Spotty feathers, Sir Barclay! It's her!"

Sir Barclay flew at top speed back onto the shed roof and strutted excitedly. "Don't worry, my dear Dame! I'll get you out! *Squawk!*"

He reappeared on my shoulder as we both tried to open the padlock, but it was no use. Worse still, Dame Genevieve couldn't even hear us because of the loud music. She hadn't flinched a feather. That was why the radio was on!

*SMASH!*

Sir Barclay and I jolted around to see Celeste standing behind us, her signature hockey stick poised for action. A multi-coloured hockey ball had smashed through a greenhouse window and flumped onto the soil between last year's wizened tomato plant roots and a discarded metal watering can.

Propped up behind a bag of compost was a pink, leather satchel. Celeste's glittery water bottle poked out the top, next to a fluffy, purple pencil case and Nan's book! Everything was now covered in shards of glass.

"And what do you think you're doing here?" Celeste demanded.

# CHAPTER SIXTEEN

## *Magic Word*

The pungent aroma of rose petals and rotting compost clung to the back of my throat. It wasn't just the smell that was making me retch. It was being face to face with an unblinking Celeste at the bottom of her enormous garden.

"I said, what are you doing here? You do know this is private property, don't you?"

As if Celeste wasn't basking in my fear enough, she repeatedly pounded the edge of her hockey stick into the palm of her hand, which in turn made mine sweaty. Normal sensation in my legs had been exchanged for jelly, and they were wobbling harder than a mango blancmange on a bouncy castle. Unless it happened to be one of Mum's homemade mango blancmanges, in which case it wouldn't wobble at all.

I wanted to answer, but the words were trapped in my mouth. I couldn't get them out.

"Reply, quickly!" A slug was slithering towards the flowerbed.

"I'm trying!" I said through gritted teeth. My mind was

racing. Everything about Celeste was making me anxious because it meant she was either going to do something mean or she was thinking about doing something mean.

"I. . . err. . . just wondered if you fancied playing out?" I lied, attempting to stop my left eye from twitching.

She studied my face as miniscule beads of sweat gathered on my top lip. This was torture.

"Why would I want to play out with you?" She finally guffawed.

The hairs on the back of my neck began to prickle, the revolting stench from the rotting compost pile covered with potato peelings and eggshells, making me feel woozy.

"Well?" she demanded.

"I wondered if you'd show me how to play hockey properly."

"Squawk! Well done, Fleur! Brilliant answer!"

My cheeks turned bright red as I tried not to draw attention to the fact that I knew Sir Barclay was watching us from a cosy hole in the middle of the conifer hedge.

"Because it's nice to learn from each other, isn't it?" I added.

"Ha! Is that so?" Celeste smirked. "Even after today's unfortunate little incident?"

I nodded without meaning to. My mind wasn't in charge of my muscles. The jelly in my legs had wobbled its way into my stomach and engulfed the rest of my body. Celeste moved closer, forcing me to walk backwards until I bumped into her shed.

"Got a bit of a shock today, did you, when you losers got covered in parrot poo? How strange! If only there'd been someone around to put a stop to it. Someone who could–oh,

I don't know–talk to animals and ask a couple of squirrels for help maybe? Any idea who that could be?"

My heart pumped so hard, I almost thought the shed would vibrate to my beat. She knew. Celeste knew I could talk to animals and not just from reading Nan's book. She had seen me talking to the two squirrels on the hockey pitch earlier. Not that they had helped.

"I don't know what you're on about," I said. "Yeah, it was a shock. It's not every day a parrot storms the school hockey pitch and poos over you, but it was just one of those weird things. I guess the bird ate something that disagreed with it."

"*Squawk*! Well done, Fleur! Keep calm, you're doing well."

Celeste laughed. "I thought you might say something like that. Lots of weird things happen when you're around, Fleur. Don't you agree?"

Yes, I did, but what would she know? It's not like she knew anything about me. She hadn't bothered to find out.

"Lots of weird things don't always happen to me," I said. "Sometimes I'm just in the wrong place at the wrong time, that's all."

Celeste screwed up her eyes, unconvinced, and walked slowly around in a circle in front of me, still holding her hockey stick.

"Is that your excuse for being in my garden? My mum won't be impressed that you've come to my house uninvited to pick on me again. You're so unkind and unwelcoming. Don't worry, Fleur, she knows all about you. I told her myself. One little shout from me and you're in big trouble!"

I clenched my fists and shook them. I wasn't the bully! She was!

"*Squawk!* Don't listen to her, Fleur! She's trying to get to you! Ignore her!"

Celeste checked her watch. "Well, lovely as this is, I must dash. Places to go, people to see, and all that. I trust you can find your own way out?"

"What about parrots to hide?" I asked, stepping towards her, fists clenched.

She narrowed her eyes. "Ha! I told you that you were weird, Fleur! I'm not the one who owns a parrot–you are–and it's only a matter of time before everyone at school finds out that you were the one behind today's poo-fest."

"Why, the little twerp!" Sir Barclay shouted from behind her. "You were right, Fleur, she's mean. Sneakily mean!"

"Can you imagine what your teammates are going to say when I tell them it was your parrot that ruined their faces and clothes?" Celeste continued.

"Why would you tell everyone that?" I asked. "That's a lie and you know it. It was your parrot all along."

"I keep telling you, Fleur. I don't own a parrot! You lot are all the same, with your special gifts that you can't figure out how to work properly. What a waste!"

"And what would you know about special gifts?"

I was desperate to wipe the know-it-all smirk off her face, but she was right, I didn't know anything about my magic, not really. I didn't know how it all worked or why I even had it, but the last time I checked, she wasn't a gift expert. Reading Nan's book and seeing me talk to two squirrels, didn't count either.

"I mean, it's not like you've got any special gifts, have you?" I added.

I was so cross I could have cried because it felt like this was life's way of teaching me a lesson. I should've told Nan about Celeste's bullying when it first started, I should never have read Nan's private notebook, and I definitely shouldn't have lost it at the pond. Then I remembered what Nan had said to me in her attic-room before tea, about not worrying about the 'what ifs' because they distracted from the here and now. I took a deep breath and another step towards Celeste.

"What would you know!" Celeste snapped. "You think you're so special, don't you? Just like Mum and Dad, and all the others I've met. Well, I don't think you're special at all. I think you're weird, and I figured you out when I first clapped eyes on you in Farrow Park getting mobbed by a load of birds!"

What? Celeste was there? Watching me? I rubbed my forehead, flummoxed, wondering why she had never before mentioned seeing me wrestle pecking birds that made my ear bleed.

"Just like I figured out there was something bothering that lame, spotty parrot I found hiding in our shed when we moved here from Italy."

"I thought you said you didn't have a parrot."

Celeste suddenly looked hot and sweaty.

"*Squawk!* That's more like it, Fleur! Play her at her own game!"

It was great knowing Sir Barclay was with me, but it wasn't the same as human protection. I wanted Nan.

"I don't own it! I found it. It was moping about in the back of the shed all alone and seemed to brighten up whenever I talked to it. I never chatted about anything heavy, just made light conversation about the weather, or hockey, or my weekend plans. I think it liked the company if I'm honest, so I gave it some nuts and water and told it I would help but only if it helped me first. Seriously, animals are so gullible. As soon as I mentioned the word Animalator that was it! It would do anything for me."

How did she know all this? I glanced at Sir Barclay who kept opening and shutting his beak in disbelief.

"I knew it would go for the bait. Birds are pretty dim. I should know because I tricked one the same way in Italy. Said I would help it if it threw a whole pizza in this annoying kid's face. I was fed up with Marco Pinto constantly showing off to the rest of my class when I lived in Italy and all it took was one slip of the magic Animalator word and, hey presto, he got what he deserved. The smile soon disappeared from his little face when it was covered with stringy mozzarella. I don't know why everyone was so into Marco. Seriously, being able to disguise yourself isn't that amazing–that's what fancy dress is for."

She cackled. Sir Barclay made his angry, whistling noise, but I shook my head without taking my eyes off Celeste. He got the hint and stayed where he was. We had to keep it together.

"What's mozzarella got to do with a pooing parrot?" I asked, frowning.

Celeste scoffed, which made me feel about two centimetres tall. "Ah, yes, the pooing parrot, I was getting to that. It was the dimmest of them all. I didn't think it would believe me so imagine my surprise when it ignored you, as instructed, and took aim. Hockey match won, and another step closer to winning the Farrow Park Cup. You see, Fleur, you magical lot aren't that special after all."

My mind exploded. Was this how Nan felt before she had a dizzy spell, because I couldn't keep up with everything that Celeste had said?

"*Squawk!* I've had quite enough of this!" This time it was Celeste who didn't have time to duck as Sir Barclay raced towards her, tucking his head forward to give him extra speed. "Move aside, Fleur! Before you get covered."

*SPLAT!*

The most enormous squirt of parrot poo flew from Sir Barclay's bottom and onto Fleur's face. Screams erupted from her as she spluttered on his rear-end surprise.

"Eugh! This is disgusting! Mum! Mum!"

I gasped in astonishment. I didn't think he had it in him. As Celeste pulled at a rhubarb leaf to help her deal with the slimy consequences, Sir Barclay plunged into the greenhouse through the shattered window and knocked over Celeste's bag.

He fished out Nan's notebook with his beak and went to fly away, but a shard of broken glass caught his foot and he shuddered in pain. He squawked and the book fell, landing on the grass beside Celeste. She heard it land and quickly smeared the leaf across her eyes so she could see. Spotting the notebook, she lunged for it.

"No way!" I leapt forward and pushed her out of the way, grabbing the book tightly with both hands and hugging it to my chest as Celeste mounted my back.

"Give it back!" she hissed. "It's staying with me."

"Not a chance!" I tried to shove her off but she had a

strong grip. "It's not yours!" I purposefully stamped on her foot with all my might.

"Aaagh!" she screamed in my ear before immediately letting go.

I looked around for Sir Barclay and spotted him right above our heads.

"Catch!" I yelled and threw Nan's book up high where he seized it in his beak and enveloped it with his claws. He disappeared and I quickly dashed to the shed. While Celeste was still holding her foot, I banged forcefully on the window. At last, Dame Genevieve faced me within her cage.

"Don't worry, Dame Genevieve, we'll get you out somehow," I shouted. "Sir Barclay will think of something."

I pressed my ear against the wood to listen and prayed that Celeste's Mum still hadn't heard the commotion outside. I knew she wouldn't be working down in the basement all night. Time was running out.

"Sir Barclay?" Dame Genevieve chirped, surprised. "You know where he is? Please help! She's moving soon, and I don't want to go with her! She promised to help me, but then she locked me in here. I thought she was an Animalator, but she isn't! Now I'm trapped!"

Soil hit the back of my head and speckled the shed window. I slowly turned around to prevent the soil from slipping further down into my hood, only to see a flustered Celeste. Her usually neat, black fringe was ruffled, and her cheeks red and damp.

"Get away from my parrot!" she said, wiping her face with her sleeve. "Nobody leaves my garden until I say so."

# CHAPTER SEVENTEEN

## *Thunder Sneeze*

Sir Barclay was nowhere to be seen. I kept checking the trees, but he had completely disappeared when I needed him most. Why couldn't I have acquired the special gift of turning back time? Being able to speak with animals wasn't much use in an empty garden, only I had forgotten–it wasn't empty.

"What are you going to do now that your feathered friend has abandoned you?"

The rhubarb leaf had been successful in mopping up the parrot poo from Celeste's face; all that was left was a chalky outline around her hair, chin, and nostrils which flared widely in my direction.

I didn't know what I was going to do. All I knew was that every ounce of my earlier braveness had seeped out of my skin thanks to Celeste's glare and intimidating hockey stick.

"Can you smell that?" Celeste quizzed as she moved around me, sniffing.

Next door's dogs began to bark uncontrollably. "It wasn't us!" they protested.

"Smell what?" I quivered. "I can't smell anything, other than your compost."

"Oh, I can smell it, Fleur. It's chicken, the scent of fear, through and through. You're a big, fat chicken who doesn't have the guts to admit what you really are."

The thumping in my ears was deafening. It was all too much. I closed my eyes and shook my head, hoping that I could shake off the wobbly fear that had gripped my entire body. A cool breeze wafted around my skin, but I knew it couldn't be Nan. The breeze brushed my arms until goosebumps exploded under my skin. I crossed my arms, rubbing my hands up and down, but it still didn't stop the cold or wobbliness.

"*Squawk!* What's happening, Fleur? Are you okay?"

Sir Barclay had reappeared, but his voice was muffled. It was as though my head was stuck in a washing machine. The thought of admitting to Celeste that I could hear animals had sent me into a juddering spin cycle. I didn't want to be weird. I didn't want any of this. I wanted to be normal Fleur Marie again.

"Aren't you going to say anything?" Celeste asked. "You've gone really quiet for someone who's trying to steal my parrot!"

The bright, peachy sky was suddenly stained with a smoky, black plume that quickly made its mark on the evening horizon. Celeste frowned as she looked up.

A few neighbouring birds squawked furiously as the swirling clouds gathered pace. Around and around they hurtled, spinning themselves into thick candyfloss knots. I coughed loudly, my throat suddenly dry and tickly. All I wanted was to feel normal again and go home to watch *Tat and That* with Mum and Nan.

*CRACK!*

A jagged fork of lightning cut through the heavy clouds.

Celeste screamed. "What's going on? Why is there lightning in the middle of summer?"

I coughed again.

*CRACK!*

A wave of electricity flashed and thunder rumbled all around us. I needed to get out of Celeste's garden, fast, before my bones or Sir Barclay's feathers got torched. I coughed again. I couldn't help it. Celeste's bottom half froze, yet her arms, shoulders, and head darted in every direction as she hunted high and low for answers.

The lightning stopped as suddenly as it had started, and the thunder trailed off, replaced with a brilliant, blue sky and baking sunshine. For 5pm in the afternoon, it was weird and frighteningly intense. My sweaty upper lip was nothing compared to the moisture that gathered on my eyelids caused by the pelting of the sun's rays.

Celeste screamed again. "Can you feel that? What's happening? It's getting even hotter. How is that possible? Mum! Mum!"

She dropped her hockey stick and covered her sweltering head with both hands as I fell wearily to my knees. The sickly feeling in my tummy persisted. I had never felt like this before, and for the first time since entering Celeste's garden, I half hoped Celeste's mum would hear.

My throat was so dry, I felt the tickling cough catching my tonsils and making them wobble. I buried my face in the crook of my arm and coughed into it.

The brightest rainbow I had ever seen appeared above our heads as the intense heat, grew even more intense.

I swallowed, sweat trickling down the back of my neck.

"Stop!" Celeste yelled.

I kept as still as possible and glanced around wondering who she was talking to, but there was only the two of us, on our knees, our faces pink and sweaty. Another cough erupted before I could stop it.

Celeste stared at me and wiped her forehead with the back of her hand. "It's you, Fleur, isn't it? You're doing it."

"Doing what?" I grimaced. I wasn't doing anything apart from clutching my tummy, and covering my mouth, desperate for whatever this was to be over.

"Just stop it!" Celeste shouted.

"I can't! I'm not doing anything!"

This wasn't happening. This wasn't happening. THIS–WAS–NOT–HAPPENING!

"You are, Fleur! You're controlling it. The weather changes every time you cough."

"No, it doesn't!" I said, shaking my head in protest.

My whole body convulsed. Pure fear overflowed from my pores. Celeste was right, this was no coincidence, but how on earth was I supposed to stop it when I didn't know how it had begun?

I rose and tried to slow my breathing. It wasn't easy but I managed to hold back a cough until it suddenly changed into. . .

*ATCHOO!*

It was the loudest, most ferocious sneeze I had ever blasted out.

Large raindrops landed on my face, one-by-one, until the heavens fully opened. The rain pelted down faster and harder than I had ever known in my life. It actually hurt!

*ATCHOO!*

This was ridiculous, but it still didn't stop. I couldn't stop any of it. Celeste covered her mouth with her hands and the colour drained from her face.

"You're a Meteolator!" she whispered.

A Meteolator? What was one of those? Nan hadn't mentioned that on her list and it wasn't hidden elsewhere in her book either.

The wind whipped our legs as we battled to stay upright in the freak storm. Rain and hailstones violently pelted the greenhouse, and I wondered how many other panes of glass had smashed in the force. Celeste's bag was completely drenched, the contents strewn across the greenhouse floor... including Nan's chess piece! It was there, I could see it, next to Celeste's sodden pencil case.

"I always knew you were weird, Fleur," Celeste shouted over the wind and the rain, which had turned her hair into a saturated mop. "But I thought it was just animals! Wait until I tell everybody at school tomorrow!"

She wouldn't, would she? I gagged because I already knew the answer to my question. Yes, she would absolutely blab, and everyone would probably believe her too.

I felt like I was going to be sick as the rain lashed my face.

"*Squawk!* Ignore her, Fleur! Talk to your nan! She'll know what to do. *Squawk!*" Sir Barclay clung to the loose felt on top of Celeste's shed, ever the protector, not wanting to leave Dame Genevieve's side.

The nauseating wave that had consumed my whole body was now reduced to nothing more than a tinny taste in my mouth.

"Tell them then!" I said calmly. "And let's see how popular you really are!"

*WHOOSH!*

One last blast of air boomed between Celeste and me, throwing us both to the ground. I found myself slumped against the shed, staring at Celeste who had taken an unfortunate tumble into a large pond next to the greenhouse.

Her bum was stuck tight to the bottom and she was unable to lift herself out. The strength of the boom, combined with her landing in the water from a great height, had created a vacuum of pressure that had sucked her into the pond full of gunk.

"I'll move then, shall I?" A small frog tutted and jumped towards the back of the greenhouse, somewhat exasperated at having to share its water space with Celeste.

"Look at the state of me! What even is this? Mum! Mum!" Celeste bellowed at the top of her lungs whilst cupping gunk in her hands.

There was no way Celeste's mum would not hear that.

The sun disappeared, the rain stopped, and the wind reverted to a gentle whisper. I twisted my arm through the greenhouse window and grabbed Nan's chess piece from the floor.

"*Squawk!* Quick, Fleur!" Sir Barclay said. "Celeste's mum is coming!"

I took one last look through the shoddy shed window. The storm had loosened a small strip of black tape at the bottom. It was only tiny, but I could see her perfectly. Dame Genevieve Ophelia Monroe Smythe sat cowering in a rusty, old birdcage at the back of the shed.

"We'll come back for you, Dame Genevieve. I promise!" I said.

"MUM!"

*CLICK! CLICK! CLICK!*

Security lights flashed on, one after the other.

"*Squawk!* Hurry up, Fleur! There's a clearing next to that tree, there. Go, and I'll meet you on the other side!"

I sprinted through the prickly gap taking one final look behind me. Sir Barclay gently kissed the taped-up window before bowing his head and flying off to the sound of Celeste's mum's footsteps.

# CHAPTER EIGHTEEN

## *Caged Animal*

It was the switching of the plugs that stirred me as Mum pulled my bedside lamp out and replaced it with the vacuum cleaner at 7am. Lucky me. It was far too early for anything, especially cleaning. My head and eyes were still throbbing from last night's confrontation with Celeste, and the revelation that in addition to being able to talk to animals, I could now also conjure up weird storms. Controlling them, however, was a different matter. It felt like they had controlled me.

I'd been bursting to speak to Nan when I got home from Celeste's, but Mum was all defensive about her again, so it was straight to bed on a school night for me. Mum even kept her bedroom door open in case Nan needed her in the night, so sneaking up the creaky attic stairs hadn't been an option either. I needed to speak to Nan urgently, so we could figure this out together. No more waiting or putting it off.

I peeped out from under my duvet and saw Mum was already dressed for work at the antiques centre and sporting her favourite umbrella scarf. She smelled lovely which was a relief, as it meant that any traces of feeling sick had gone. My head still felt a little fuzzy though, and every time I moved my tongue, I tasted metal.

"Come on, love, hop to it or you'll be late." She dragged the vacuum cleaner across my carpet. "No time for porridge this morning, you'll have to make do with toast."

That was fine by me! I threw my duvet back and leapt out of bed, which made my head thump faster. I couldn't afford to hang about or feel groggy, I needed to see Nan and re-group with Sir Barclay. Every second wasted meant we were further away from rescuing Dame Genevieve.

"I'll make it up to you though!" Mum turned the vacuum off and cupped my face in her hands, playfully squashing my cheeks. "I'll make us something special for tea, instead. It's a beautiful day. A day made for jerk chicken and goats' cheese quiche!"

Bleurgh! No day was ever made for Mum's jerk chicken and goats' cheese quiche because she never seasons them right. Nan's jerk chicken was the best.

"Alright then," I said hesitantly as I hotfooted it to the bathroom with my uniform tucked under my armpit.

I suppose you could say last night was a mini triumph because Sir Barclay had retrieved Nan's book, and I had grabbed Nan's chess piece before running home. Neither of us had wanted to leave Dame Genevieve behind, but what choice did we have? Stick around and get arrested for trespassing? Or exposed as common thieves and weather weirdos by Celeste and her mum? No thanks.

It wasn't easy leaving Dame Genevieve alone in Celeste's shed. It was heart-breaking. I still had the vision of Sir Barclay painfully saying goodbye to her etched in my mind. The only comfort was that they had seen each other, and Dame Genevieve knew we would go back for her as soon as possible.

Sir Barclay barely spoke on the way home other than to tell me he had replaced Nan's book back down the side of her armchair. That's where he had disappeared to!

By the time my mind had stopped fizzing and worrying, it was after midnight. The last thing I remembered was Sir Barclay's scratchy beak pecking my forehead, which I think was a goodnight kiss.

"*Squawk!* There you are. Good of you to join us!" he announced now, poking his feathery face through the crack of the bathroom window after I had showered and dressed. He didn't sound particularly happy, and I didn't blame him. "*Squawk!* I've been trying to wake you all night. Honestly, Fleur, you sleep like the dead."

"Wake me? Why? What's the matter? Is it Nan?"

"*Squawk!* No, she's fine but I've been thinking you've got to tell your nan about last night. She's the only one who can truly help you understand your gifts because I haven't got a magical feather in my body. I was worried about you, Fleur. You were vulnerable and distressed in Celeste's garden, and it wasn't nice to see."

I slowly plaited my hair, strangely receptive to Sir Barclay's words of wisdom.

"*Squawk!* And I don't care how strong you think you are; you can't afford to put yourself in another dangerous situation. We can't keep doing this alone."

I buried my face deep into my towel. Old fluff-pants and I were finally on the same wavelength. I agreed, but there was so much to tell Nan that she didn't yet know, like the bullying,

Dame Genevieve, Celeste knowing stuff not written in her book, and that was without my additional weather gift. What if telling her was too much? Could I really risk confessing everything so soon after she got out of hospital? I couldn't bear for her to be poorly again, especially if it was all my fault.

"I will. Anyway, how are you doing?"

I could tell from Sir Barclay's neck swoop that he was agitated, and who could blame him? His wife was locked in a shed!

"*Squawk!* Well, when I couldn't wake you last night, I was going to fly straight back to Celeste's garden to rescue Dame Genevieve."

"What? How? You mean, you went there all by yourself? Without me?" I tried to hide my disappointment by folding my towel and tucking it gently back over the radiator.

"*Squawk!* As it turns out, some nincompoop decided to close your nan's window while she was fast asleep and before I had a chance to fly out. I've been cooped up in this house all night, right up until your mum woke your nan a few minutes ago."

"I didn't shut it!" I protested.

"*Squawk!* You don't need to tell me that. An earthquake measuring 9.2 on the Richter scale wouldn't have woken you last night," he said. "It was your mother. I'm sure her intentions were admirable, but I've been trapped in this house all night like some kind of caged animal! It's outrageous!"

It was outrageous, but it was also a teeny, tiny bit amusing. After the seriousness of the last few days, it was nice to have something to smile about, if only for a second.

"So, what now?" I asked. "Shall we head over to Celeste's

house together and skip school? I could go in late. Say I had a dentist appointment or something?"

We had to rescue Dame Genevieve before Celeste hid her somewhere else. There were suddenly two things which made the prospect of revisiting Celeste's house with Sir Barclay more appealing than last night:

1. Celeste wouldn't be there. Her mum would never let her miss school in case it interfered with her important work meetings.
2. I'd miss the final school hockey practice before tomorrow's tournament—yippee!

"*Squawk!* I don't think that's such a good idea, do you?"

"Are you kidding? I think it's a brilliant idea! Do you want Dame Genevieve back or not?"

"*Squawk!* I'm just saying that some time to recover from your ordeal last night might be best." Sir Barclay clicked his beak anxiously. "You need to look after yourself, Fleur. You'll be no good to Dame Genevieve if you're sick. I don't want you following in your nan's footsteps. I assure you that you'll be more help if you keep an eye on Celeste at school and make sure she doesn't sneak back home."

I unlocked the bathroom door dejectedly. While it was lovely to know he cared about me, there was no way I was going straight to school. Fuzzy head or otherwise.

"I don't like it, but I will if I must!" I said convincingly.

He bowed his head with gratitude, which made me feel bad.

"*Squawk!* Good girl, Fleur. Save your strength for today's practice match and tomorrow's tournament. Celeste's too much of a loose cannon. She could be up to anything, and you'll be best placed at school to find out what that is! Squawk!"

I could tell by the way Mum knocked on the door that her chirpiness was at risk if I didn't get a move on.

"I'm coming!" I shouted.

"So is Christmas!" she retorted.

I opened the bathroom door ready to make a hasty departure when Nan called me from the attic. Mum conveniently appeared on the landing with a pile of clean bedding destined for the airing cupboard.

"Just a minute, Nan!"

"Don't go bothering her, Fleur," Mum whispered. "She might think she's invincible, but she's not. She's really very frail. The clouds frightened her last night. I don't know what she was looking for at the other side of Farrow Park, but something in the sky spooked her."

"Please, Mum, I'll be two minutes then straight to school," I begged.

Mum sighed. "You've got one minute, and I've already started counting."

"Coming, Nan!"

I darted up the stairs as fast as my tired legs would let me; they were still a little weak after last night. Nan was sitting in bed reading her newspaper with her reddy-orangey notebook resting on her knee.

**POLICE GREEN SLIPPER TRIUMPH!**

The headline was splashed across the front page of the newspaper. Of course, the lack of 'Nan sightings' hadn't got anything to do with the police's involvement. She was simply too poorly to fly and make mischief, but they didn't know that.

She looked up from her paper. "There you are! Are you all ready to knock 'em dead at today's last practice match?"

I was ready to knock something, but Dame Genevieve was the main priority; Celeste would have to wait.

"We'll see," I said, distracted. "They're a tough team to beat."

"Nasty tricks often are," she said, putting down her paper. "But you'll find a way through. You're a beautiful, kind and intelligent girl, Fleur. One your mum and I can be proud of."

I rubbed my thumb along the edge of my jaw. I had heard someone say something like that before, 'one to be proud of'. Maybe I was more tired after last night than I realised because I couldn't remember who had said it. I stifled a yawn, keen to concentrate fully on Nan.

"All you need to do is be true to yourself and face your fears and your feelings. Face them head on like a storm."

I raised my eyebrows. Why did she mention a storm? She flashed me a funny look, which was more of a glare with an accompanying twitch. She knew! I should've realised when Mum mentioned her being frightened by the clouds. I tapped my foot excitedly.

"Remember to keep yourself in check, today, won't you?" Nan pressed.

"How do you mean?" I asked.

She smiled. Her smile always made me feel better. "What I mean is, if something's bothering you, then tell people how you feel. Don't fall into the same trap as your father, because if you keep bottling things up, your body will react in a way that even you didn't know was possible."

What? My brain suddenly froze. If it was a computer screen it would have turned blue with weird white writing on it while it decided whether to refresh. I sat on Nan's footstool because I felt bogged-down.

What traps did Dad fall into? He left because he was depressed after Grandpa Willie died. Not because he was getting bullied or hearing animals or controlling the weather or was he?

Nan knowingly tapped her book with a black pen and waited for me to react. Now was the time to tell her. She wanted me to tell her! She might be frail, but she wasn't daft–why else would she have mentioned feelings and storms? I had already sensed that the two might be somehow connected.

I took a deep breath. "Okay, so, here's the thing. Strange things have been happening to me, I can. . . I can hear animals, but then I found out last night that I did something, somehow, to the weather. I'm sure of it, Nan, but I can't explain it."

Nan's eyes lit up. "I'm all ears and so proud of you for being brave and finally talking to me."

"I'm sorry it's taken so long," I said. "You see, it started with this new girl, Celeste. She's been picking on me at school, and then I heard Sir Barclay talk and–hang on a minute, you just said you're proud. It reminded me of something someone said last night! She said something about being one to be proud of."

Nan leant forward, completely foxed. "Who said something last night, baby? And where?"

"At Celeste's house. It was her mum. She said she wanted her to act like a proper. . . "

"A proper what, Fleur? What is it? You can tell me, it's fine."

I clasped my hands together and put them behind my head, raising my elbows to think. What was the funny word she used?

"Time's up, Fleur!" Mum said from the landing.

"Hexter!" I whispered. "That's what she said. That it was time Celeste acted like a proper Hexter. What's a Hexter?"

"A Hexter is someone who has magic." Nan smiled at me. "Like you."

# CHAPTER NINETEEN

## *Suitcases*

I had never eaten a piece of toast so fast. I had to get to Celeste's house. After kissing Mum goodbye, I hurried out the front door and retraced my steps back to Celeste's. My tummy wasn't tight like it had been before, but the adrenaline bubbling inside me, made me want to run faster, as opposed to being sick. I now had another new name to get used to, not just Fleur Marie Bottom, or an Animalator, or even a Meteolator–both of which still felt unreal–but now a Hexter too.

I squeezed back through the same prickly bush as I did last night, only in reverse. I shuffled through the undergrowth, head down, and couldn't hear a thing other than the sound of my own feet which scuffed the dry soil underneath. As Celeste's shed came into view my tummy lurched warily.

The whole garden was deserted. I checked for signs of Celeste and other voices, but the coast was clear. I crept to the shed door, gently stroking the wood as I went. It was open. The padlock was discarded on the floor next to it.

"*Squawk!*"

"Aaagh!"

We flapped arms and wings at the same time.

"*Squawk!* Whatever happened to letting yourself recover?"

"Whatever happened to us not doing things alone?" I retorted.

Sir Barclay's eyes looked desperately empty. I couldn't be cross with him. He only wanted Dame Genevieve back, but it didn't look likely from the hollow shed around us which had been stripped bare.

He pecked the floor sadly. His slight frame looked helpless and lost.

"Where is she?" I asked. "Did you see anything?"

"*Squawk!* The rotten shed was empty by the time I arrived. Everyone's already gone to work, along with a fleet of removal vans. There are only a few rooms with boxes and suitcases in, and no sign of Dame Genevieve anywhere. *Squawk!* All I found in here was this."

Sir Barclay pulled out a small red feather from underneath his wing with Dame Genevieve's signature spots on it.

"*Squawk!* She's gone, and now this is all I have left of her." Sir Barclay bowed his head and tucked the feather back under his wing for comfort. "We were so close, Fleur, but now it feels like we're further away from finding her than we've ever been."

I tiptoed along the busy corridor and reached the lockers only two minutes after the panpipes chimed. I had made it and without rousing suspicion. School was crazy! Everyone was excited about the last two days of term, especially everyone in my class because we were less than forty-eight hours away from finishing primary school forever! I didn't know how I felt. Petrified? Excited? Nervous? I settled on a mixture of all three.

As I swapped my bag for my hockey gear, I noticed a furtive Celeste through the library window, pacing back and forth. She looked pale and agitated, and was deep in conversation on her mobile phone, which should've been locked away in Mr Augustus's drawer straight after the bell. She didn't see me sneak in, and judging by the miserable look on her face, the conversation wasn't going to plan.

"What do you mean we're staying in a hotel tonight? I thought we weren't flying out until Saturday. I've still got a suitcase to finish packing. Why do we always have to move to a new house just as I've started to settle in?"

I could see her through the bookshelves, grinding her teeth.

"No, Mum." She sighed. "It's not that I don't like the idea of America. I've got a really important hockey tournament tomorrow and... yes... yes, it is. It's the final. Tomorrow. I did tell you about it. Yes, I know you've got to work. Of course, I like New York cheesecake, and the Guggenheim Art Gallery sounds brilliant, but do we really have to go tomorrow night? I mean, we usually live somewhere for at least a year before we move again, and... well... can't we stay a few more months? I like it here."

I suddenly felt awkward earwigging into her private conversation. It wasn't right, and she obviously didn't want anyone to hear what was going on at home, otherwise she wouldn't be lurking about in the library alone. Unless it was because she was worried her phone would get confiscated if she used it in class, but I doubted it.

She ended the call abruptly and launched her phone towards the bean bags where it landed on the grubby, blue fabric. I held my breath for as long as I could, hoping she wouldn't hear me, but as I exhaled my nose let out a funny squeak.

Celeste's hair whipped around faster than Mr Augustus's wig on a rollercoaster.

"What are you doing here?" she barked. "Have you been listening to me the whole time? There are laws against that, you know!"

"No, I wasn't listening at all," I lied. "Mr Augustus asked me to come and find you. He said we needed to get ready for our final hockey practice."

My legs gently trembled. Another storm was the last thing I needed. I was determined not to let her get to me like she had done last night, because I was beginning to think there was more to Celeste than I realised. More than anyone realised, and if what Nan said was true, then I wasn't the only Hexter in the library.

"Oh, did he really?" she snarled. "Well, perhaps I should check that out for myself. And while I'm there, maybe I should warn him about your nasty coughs and sneezes. Wouldn't want him losing his wig in sudden bad weather now, would we?"

I had to agree with her about Mr Augustus's wig, it was a liability, but her threats towards me were becoming old news now. A bit like flying arms and slippers in the *Evening Gazette*.

"What's your problem?"

"My problem, Fleur, is you! I don't understand how you

get a special gift when you're the least special person I know. You haven't got a clue! Take last night, what even was that? And don't say 'nothing' because it was all written down in that book. I saw it. Only your irritating parrot pinched it from me!"

"You can't pinch something that's already yours," I said factually. "Sir Barclay was simply reclaiming it."

Ha! Check me out! Celeste frothed at the mouth. A bit like one of those science experiments you do with a mint and cola.

"You might not want everyone knowing about your weird animal conversations and magic tricks, but I think our class would be extremely interested to hear all about them."

She didn't have a clue that I had overheard her mum call her a Hexter, and now thanks to Nan, I knew exactly what a Hexter was.

"If you want everyone in our class to think you've gone bonkers, Celeste, then be my guest, tell them about my powers. It's not like you've got any proof."

With Nan's book now safely back in her possession, Celeste didn't have a leg to stand on, although she did still have Dame Genevieve somewhere, so I had to be careful.

Celeste clasped her hands in front of her, enraged. I had finally stood up to her!

Celeste scoffed. "If you want to make this a popularity contest, then be my guest, but I think you're setting yourself up for a huge fall."

I knew it wouldn't be long before her miserable face turned smug and mean again. Now what was I supposed to do? I spotted her mobile phone nestled on top of the bean bags, and boom, there it was.

"I'm pretty sure your popularity will fade once everyone finds out you're flying to another country soon."

She marched her newly flustered pink cheeks over to the beanbags in the corner and retrieved her phone.

"It's none of your business where I'm going on Friday, but wherever it is, rest assured I'll be taking my parrot with me!" She smirked. Her cheeks returned to normal as she regained control of our spat. Poor Dame Genevieve. Where had she put her? And was Celeste only hanging on to her to spite me?

"Do Anais and Ruby know you're abandoning them for America?" I asked. "Or the rest of your yellow team? I wonder how well they'll take to news of you moving. It could be a terrible distraction from tomorrow's hockey tournament, don't you think?"

"You wouldn't dare!" she shrieked. "They won't believe you anyway!"

"So, you honestly think that me being able to magically create a storm with a sneeze and a splutter, or have a chit-chat with a bunch of animals, is more believable than you being shipped off to America? Not likely," I said.

"Girls!" The library door catapulted open to reveal an irate Mr Augustus, wearing a mustard-coloured tracksuit and matching headband, his wig precariously tucked in at the sides. "On the field now, before I cancel tomorrow's tournament altogether."

That sounded far too good to be true.

Mr Augustus's whistle penetrated deep into my ears and

sent everyone into a mad panic, including me. There wasn't a bird or a squirrel, or when I thought about it, any other type of animal in sight as the trees and the sky were deserted. If only the same was true of the hockey pitch, which disappointingly was full of anxious reds and eager yellows.

Celeste had already whacked the ball up the pitch towards the top goal where Anais and Ruby were diligently waiting for their next Celeste command. They both looked more jittery than usual.

I jogged over to them, praying that my ankles would survive the next twenty minutes as tensions had mounted between Celeste and I in the library. The mood felt pensive amongst the reds and yellows too. This was our final practice before tomorrow's match, and whoever won would automatically play against another school for the prestigious Farrow Park Cup.

"Hi," I said timidly, as Anais and Ruby waited for the next slice of Celeste action. It had been ages since we had last talked just the three of us. I still missed what we'd had.

"What's up with you?" Anais asked. "You look tired."

It was hard to tell if she was being concerned or insulting.

"Oh, I had a bit of a late night looking after Nan, that's all."

"Is she okay?" Ruby asked, seemingly interested. But without waiting for me to answer, she said, "Quick, Anais! She's on her way!" She was too busy hawking Celeste's every move. They both had their eyes glued to Celeste's shuffling feet, which were advancing towards us.

"Easy on the tackles, girls!" Mr Augustus shouted.

It was nice of him to notice the foul play for once, as Celeste's hockey stick 'mysteriously' wrapped its hook around Lydia's ankle bone. Celeste hurtled towards us, and Ruby swayed her bent knees as if ready to pounce whenever Celeste clicked her fingers.

"Have you two got anything nice planned this weekend then?" I asked. "Given it's the first days of total freedom?" They didn't know I was referring to freedom from Celeste as opposed to freedom from school.

It would be here before I knew it. Less than two days to go until she was on a plane, jetting away from this place and more importantly, jetting away from me. Ruby and Anais were none the wiser.

"Oh, something fun, I reckon. We'll probably hang out at Celeste's," Ruby said.

Ha! That's what she thought.

"Oh, right of course," I replied.

Nothing would have given me greater pleasure than to tell Ruby and Anais the truth about their new bestie, but it wasn't my place to say anything. Plus, unlike them, I wasn't mean.

"Has Leena put you up to this? Are you trying to put us off?" Ruby scolded. "Because we're trying to win our practice here, and we will be winning the match tomorrow too. It's like Celeste keeps telling us–we're committed, we're focused, we're–"

Anais dug an elbow in her ribs. "Get ready!"

Celeste was on her way towards us, trying to outsmart Leena who was fast on her trail. She hit the ball to Ruby, except Ruby was too busy glancing at me, and by the time she turned back towards the action, it was too late. The ball rolled past her. Leena snatched it and hit it towards Beau who swung it.

*GOAL!*

"You're useless, Ruby!" Celeste roared. "You gave it away!"

"Sorry, Celeste. I got distracted. Won't happen again." Ruby glowered at me.

In contrast, Anais wouldn't look at me. It wasn't my fault they missed Celeste's instruction. I was only making polite conversation. Why did I bother? They were just as bad as Celeste.

My eyes began to sting. That same horrible wave of sickly, prickly heat travelled through my body and up to my head. I didn't deserve to be treated this way, and as tears trickled through my eyelashes, I felt my body overcome with wobbliness. Not another storm, not again, and not at school. How on earth was I supposed to get out of this one?

# CHAPTER TWENTY

## *Tied Laces*

Clouds suddenly appeared from nowhere. They quickly turned the clear sky heavy, dark grey, forming a thick blanket of fog against the sun. Everyone rubbed their arms to compensate for the sudden loss of heat. Celeste stopped to look at me.

Not again! I'd give anything to stop it.

"Pack it in, Fleur! I'm freezing. Don't make me tell everyone about last night's storm."

Ruby and Anais frowned at each other.

"There wasn't a storm last night, was there?" Anais whispered to Ruby.

Ruby shook her head before staring at Celeste, puzzled.

"I don't remember one either," I said blankly, which must have infuriated her even more because she scrunched up her nose.

Everyone continued playing around us.

I wracked my brains, trying to remember if Nan had said anything that might prove useful. Only, everything Nan had tried to chat about lately involved my fears and my feelings. Was that it? Had Nan been trying to warn me all along? And

I'd missed it? Maybe the way out of my problems was to free up my mind and gain control of my body. How does anyone even do that? Exercise? Sleep? Meditation?

I tried to calm down and get a grip. I didn't have time for full-blown meditation, so I closed my eyes, and counted to ten instead. It often worked for Mum.

"1. . . 2. . . 3. . . "

Deep breath in, deep breath out. It was harder than it sounded. How could anyone relax on a hockey pitch with Celeste lurking nearby?

"4. . . 5. . . "

Heavy footsteps rang in my ears as everyone raced towards me, but I tried my best to ignore them.

"6. . . 7. . . "

My neck was clammy, and I felt sick, just as I had in Celeste's garden. How was that even possible when I was supposed to be counting and relaxing?

"8. . . 9. . . where are all you creatures and animals now? I could really do with some help," I muttered. The clouds drifted apart and gradually thinned. "10. Fleur Marie's coming, ready or not." I opened my eyes.

"You okay, love?" a hefty looking crow said from a nearby tree.

I looked across and spotted a further two crows and a long row of starlings. At last, extra pairs of eyes! They might not be Sir Barclay's, but maybe they would do.

"I know it's a lot to ask," I whispered, making sure the others couldn't hear, "but that girl on her own over there has been really mean to me, and I've had enough. She's got something that belongs to me and won't give it back." I gestured my head in Celeste's direction, so he knew exactly who I was talking about. "Don't suppose you can help?"

"I know the one," he said gruffly. "I've seen her before, always hooking ankles and whacking kids with her stick. Leave it with me, I'll see what I can do."

He disappeared towards the other birds and they all huddled together. Seconds later the crows nosedived towards a large, empty equipment sack by the side of the pitch that usually held cones and bibs. They picked the bag up using their beaks and claws and dropped it straight on top of Celeste's head. Now was my chance.

Celeste screamed but her voice was muffled by the scratchy material.

"Where have you put your parrot?" I said through gritted teeth before the others moved closer.

"None of your business, weirdo! Now get this off me before I tell Mr Augustus! He's already on my side and you know it."

Ruby and Anais rushed over to help her and tried to lift the bag up. I nodded at the crows to thank them, then quickly joined in with the game as everyone trotted towards us. Mr Augustus shook his head at Ruby and Anais and wagged his finger as they looked on horrified. Emi took charge of the ball, showing no sympathy for Celeste's bag predicament, and skilfully tapped it into the goal.

"Yes!" Emi shouted as she ran towards a group of cheering reds.

Mr Augustus's whistle acknowledged the score. "Well done, reds! Let's play on though, quickly! We haven't got long left before science. Stop messing about with bags you three and get back to it!"

He pointed again at Ruby and Anais who were still trying to prise Celeste's head out of the bag. I held back but hovered near them, not wanting to miss any of the action.

"I'm not messing about!" Celeste screamed, but Mr Augustus had already followed the others down the pitch and didn't hear.

Anais and Ruby finally managed to set her free, but then they screamed and jumped backwards when the menacing crows darted from the tree, hurtling orange cones at Celeste's feet. Celeste didn't have time to catch her balance. She tripped over the cones and plummeted to the ground. Everyone laughed out loud.

"Over to you now, lads," one of the crows said to six tiny starlings who hopped out from behind the same tree and headed for Celeste's laces.

Celeste lay face down and dazed on the floor, with Anais and Ruby crouched beside her, checking if she was alright, when Sir Barclay shot out of nowhere.

"Oh no!" Ruby said.

Ruby and Anais closed their eyes and covered their heads, not realising it wasn't Dame Genevieve and they weren't about to get pooed on.

"*Squawk!* I'll see to this if you don't mind!"

The starlings dispersed. Sir Barclay quickly pulled Celeste's laces without her noticing and tied them in a knot before he flew off.

Celeste rolled onto her back and nudged her friends to signal that the coast was clear. Spitting with rage at losing precious time, Celeste sprang up, eager to retrieve the ball and get back to scoring.

*THUD!*

Her time upright was short-lived as she found herself face-first in the grass once more.

"My trainers! Something's wrong with my laces! Why are they tied together? Fleur, this is you, isn't it?" Celeste yelled.

Ruby and Anais both shook their heads.

"Fleur's over there." Anais pointed at me.

*WHACK!*

Seeing another window of opportunity, Leena from our red team, hijacked the ball from Jane on Celeste's team, and passed it straight to Beau, who then knocked it over to Suki.

*GOAL!*

That was 2-0 to the reds. It had never been 2-0 to the reds!

Mr Augustus blew his whistle to end the final practice before the tournament and shooed the helpful birds away. Celeste scrabbled to fix her laces and stood up; her face livid.

"That's all we've got time for I'm afraid, girls. Well done to the reds, magnificent teamwork."

"They haven't won! That's not fair." Celeste turned a vibrant shade of beetroot and flung her arms in the air like a spoilt brat.

"Don't worry, Celeste, there's still tomorrow's final match to enjoy. One last game before we know which team will be representing us at the Farrow Park Cup."

Having never been fussed about hockey before, I suddenly had a strange urge to win. Why should the yellows always get everything?

"But the bag! The cones and my trainers! Didn't you see anything?" When Mr Augustus and the other girls looked at Celeste blankly, she pointed at me. "It was Fleur!"

Everyone walked past Celeste shaking their heads. I winked at her when nobody was looking. The clouds were swirling again and Celeste looked up alarmed. I didn't know what I was most chuffed with, the fact that I had talked to animals and outsmarted Celeste, or that the reds had won and nobody apart from me or the birds had seen how.

Celeste glared at me before she turned on Ruby and Anais.

"How could you let them beat us? I knew you weren't concentrating!"

"We're sorry, Celeste," Anais said. "We wanted to help you! We promise we'll try harder. Shall we come around to yours after school tonight and sharpen our techniques?"

"What a good idea," I said. I smiled, knowing full well Celeste would be in a hotel.

"I can't do tonight," Celeste stuttered. "Mum's. . . err. . . got to work late."

Ruby and Anais glanced at each other, deflated.

"It's fine though," Celeste said quickly. "We can practice at break and lunchtime instead and leave Fleur to clean up the boring library." She ushered them both back to the classroom smirking.

I bashed my hockey stick into the ground and spotted Sir Barclay plonked on the blue bin.

"Meet you at home later," I said. "I'm telling Nan everything."

# CHAPTER TWENTY-ONE

## *Horseradish Confessions*

"Are we all ready?" Mum asked. She was flapping the tea towel around in the kitchen trying to level out the smoke which swirled through to me and Nan in the dining room.

"We can hardly wait." Nan cheekily rolled her eyes and stuck her tongue out pretending to gag.

Poor Mum. She really was a dreadful cook, but every recipe she attempted was at least made with love.

"What did you say, Nell? I can't hear you properly. I've got the fan on."

"Sounds more enticing than the pan on," Nan chuckled.

She was trying her best to make me laugh, but it wasn't working. I was nervous about telling Nan everything, especially the part about Celeste knowing I had special gifts.

"You're quiet tonight. Is everything okay? How was hockey?" Nan asked.

"It was alright, thanks," I said. "Actually, it was better than alright. We won our practice."

I had also successfully used my Animalation gift, which felt good, but it didn't feel right to mention it out loud.

"Ta-da! That's fantastic!" Mum said. "Here's something to help celebrate. Come on, pass me your plates." Mum proceeded to dish out the revolting-looking jerk chicken and goats' cheese quiche. It had bubbled over the pastry edges and caramelised, which was code for 'rock hard–do not eat.'

"Congratulations!" Nan said, raising an eyebrow at me because we both knew eating Mum's quiche was no way to celebrate anything.

"Eat up, Fleur. You'll need your strength for tomorrow's tournament and your last day in primary school."

I wasn't quite ready for tomorrow just yet, and the thought of it still made my head spin. I mean, it was exciting to think we now stood a chance of winning, but that was only because I had used my gifts.

"Thanks," I said, testing the quiche with my fork. "I really hope it wasn't a one-off."

"Why would it be?" Mum asked.

I shrugged, then shot Nan a knowing glance as she paused chewing.

"I'll be with you for two o'clock," Mum continued, oblivious. "Mr Bowland said I can finish early, so your Nan and I will be there to watch you, with bells on. Are you excited? Ooh, I am! Your last day of primary school, and what better way to finish it than surrounded by your fellow teammates."

I nervously cleared my throat. They weren't all my teammates. Nan stared at me and swallowed.

"Cindy, I couldn't trouble you for some horseradish sauce, could I? I think it would complement the goats' cheese perfectly."

Mum eagerly walked back to the kitchen where she scoured the cupboards for Nan's horseradish sauce.

"Right, baby, be quick, what's happened? I've been worried about you since this morning. Since you asked me about Hexters and mentioned this girl Celeste picking on you."

I didn't know if it was thinking about everything that had happened this week or the relief of finally confiding in a person rather than a parrot, but tears welled in my eyes.

"Tell me what you can, baby. It's okay." Nan instantly produced a clean hanky from her sleeve and leant back on her chair to check that Mum hadn't heard us.

"It's Celeste, Nan! She's horrible! She's turned Ruby and Anais against me and won't leave my ankles alone during hockey. I'm done with being bruised! And then there's the constant voices because I can hear animals talk! It started with Sir Barclay. He's been helping me, and I've helped him find his wife in return." The truth fell from my mouth so rapidly my brain struggled to keep up. "And we found her, Nan. Dame Genevieve was in Celeste's shed, because Celeste tricked her to poo on us to be mean and win a match and prove a point that, just because I've got a gift, it doesn't make me special. But then I sneezed, and it rained, and she fell in her pond."

I took a moment to wipe my nose as Mum obliviously banged and clanged in the kitchen hunting out the horseradish sauce.

"I can't find it anywhere, Nell!" Mum yelled. "Are you sure it's in the cupboard?"

"It's in there somewhere, keep looking. Perhaps try the fridge."

"Celeste muttered a load of things about magic that weren't in your book," I continued. "Then we found your book and ran home. Now Celeste knows I can do weird stuff and is threatening to tell everyone, but she won't tell us where Dame Genevieve is. I think it's to punish me for having gifts. Which means we'll never find her again because she's moving to America tomorrow, and it's all my fault!"

"It's no use, I still can't find it," Mum said as she poked her head through from the kitchen and into the dining room. "You two carry on eating, and I'll nip across the road to the shops. Oh, my, Fleur! What's the matter, are you okay?"

I nodded and wiped my nose. "It's just the spices," I said, pretending to cough. "They went up my nose the wrong way, that's all. I'm fine." I fiddled with my sleeve and looked to Nan for help.

"The same happened to me last time we had this quiche too," Nan said, handing me a small glass of water to sip. "It's delicious though, got a lovely kick to it! I'll see to Fleur, love, if you're sure you don't mind nipping over the road."

Mum gently slapped her forehead with her palm. "Ah, sorry! I'll be more careful with the cayenne pepper next time; I must've added a pinch too much. I won't be long!" She slammed the back door behind her as she left.

Nan nodded for me to continue and comfortingly squeezed my arm.

"If I only knew how to make my gifts work properly, then maybe I could've rescued Dame Genevieve last night. Oh, it's rubbish, Nan! I've been wanting to talk to you about everything for ages, but I was too embarrassed and scared because of your dizzy spells, and I don't want you to go back to hospital again. Why can't everything just go back to being normal?"

"Shh, take a deep breath and count to ten. Everything is always okay in the end. I promise." Nan put her wrinkled hand on top of mine. "Tell me about your sneezes and the weather. You can tell me everything, you know. I'll believe you."

My tears disappeared. Even Mum's quiche didn't seem that bad anymore.

"I know you'll believe me because you already know about my special gifts, don't you?"

Nan's eyes were the largest I had ever seen, full of life and twinkle. She nodded. "And you know all about me and my book, don't you?"

"I'm sorry, Nan," I whispered. "How did you know I had it?"

"I didn't until I watched you and Sir Barclay run off together before tea last night. You didn't go to Ruby's house at all, did you?" I shook my head sheepishly. "I could tell you were up to something, and I was proved right when I spotted those strange storm clouds. Totally isolated they were, and just behind Farrow Park in the exact same direction that you both headed. I was so worried, I almost flew out to see you for myself, but I'm still too weak so I had to stay put. When I saw Sir Barclay fly towards my window, I pretended to be asleep. I saw him drop my book back down my armchair before he flew off again. The fact that you weren't with him until later, confirmed my suspicions that you both had something to do with it. Was I wrong?"

I shook my head. "I'm sorry, Nan, I know it was wrong of me to read it."

She smiled. Her skin looked as delicate as crepe paper. "I'm not worried about whether you've read my silly, scruffy notes, Fleur. They're to help me remember things in my old age, that's all. My only concern is for you."

The bumping of my heart finally slowed down. Things felt better already.

"Tell me though, do these strange things only happen when Celeste is around?"

"Just the weather control," I replied. "I can hear Sir Barclay and the other animals whether Celeste is around or not."

I waited for her to process what I had shared before asking anything else.

"I don't get why I'm suddenly a Hexter, Nan. What does it all mean? I feel weird."

"You're not in the slightest bit weird, baby. You're simply wired differently, that's all. Rest assured, Fleur, we're not odd, or weird, or strange. We're *special*."

"I don't feel particularly special."

"That's because you've not figured out how to control things properly yet, but you will. Just like I did the first time I found myself at the top of our neighbour's tree. Why do you think I've been so keen for you to talk to me? Because bottling things up isn't good for anyone, let alone for someone with special gifts. It only makes everything ten times worse if you do, and remember, I've had longer than you to understand."

"Did you always know I was magic? That I was a Hexter?" I moved some curly strands of hair behind my ear and waited patiently.

"Ever since you were a baby, I always looked for signs of magic, but I never saw it. Not once, and believe me, I watched you closely but without being too obvious because your father was so sensitive to it."

"What?" I gasped. "Does that mean Dad's a Hexter too?"

Nan nodded. "But he didn't feel like a true Hexter because his gifts didn't appear for years, which is why he wanted me to leave you alone, and leave our magic alone, because he felt like a failure. He felt as though our magic had only ever brought him disappointment."

I lurched forwards in my chair.

"Why? What did it do to him? Should I be worried?" I bit the inside of my lip and looked at Nan for answers.

Nan shook her head and smiled. "Our magic isn't anything to be afraid of, baby, it just takes time to get used to and understand. It took me a long time to realise that magic can't be rushed. It won't appear just because you want it to or because you're waiting for it, however hard you search for it or hope. It only develops when the time is right and when your body is ready."

"So what's the deal with Dad?" I asked, frowning over my cold quiche. "Was his body not ready or something?"

"Your father was desperate for his magical gifts to appear. He'd spent a lifetime watching me float out of windows and listening to my stories about who had what gifts. He was fascinated, but that soon turned to resentment and anger when nothing happened. That's why he made me promise never to tell you or your mum that I was a Hexter, or that he could be a Hexter. But you can't just stop magic or make it disappear, Fleur, that's not how it works.

"So, that's why you never told me? Because you were keeping a promise to Dad, all this time?"

"Yes, but I don't blame him. I love him and he had his reasons that I had to respect. I still do in fact, but it's different now because your gifts are finally here, only he isn't. You've got me to guide you through everything instead."

"I don't understand how to control any of it though. It just happens."

"When did it start? Can you remember something which might've given it a kick?"

I thought for a minute. "Not that I can think of. One day everything was normal and the next I woke up able to hear Sir Barclay."

"Did you fall, baby? Hurt yourself? Had a shock that you weren't expecting?"

I thought again. "The biggest shock I had was meeting Celeste. Although as it turns out, she'd already met me but decided not to introduce herself."

"I don't understand."

"I mean, she was at Farrow Park before I knew who she was, watching me get bombarded by animals and pecked to pieces by a bird. Do you know she didn't do or say anything to help? Why would she just watch in silence and then tell me afterwards she was there? It's odd."

"Some people are just born rude. Maybe that's all there is to it."

"Maybe, but the way she watches me and glares at me at school, really winds me up. It's off-putting having someone monitoring your movements all the time."

"Ah well." Nan blushed. "I find the key to watching others is to secretly do it from your own window with a telescope and not get found out!"

I giggled. I was pretty sure Celeste didn't have a telescope of her own.

"I think they're both connected," Nan said.

"What, Celeste being rude and mean?"

"No, well, yes, in a way. I think Celeste's sudden arrival and you getting badly pecked are related. Both will have caused unfamiliar shocks to the system–one emotional, and the other physical. A sort of peck-reaction that stirred up the natural gifts that were within you all along but were taking their time to come out."

Hmm. I took another moment to think but tried to hurry. Mum would be back any minute because the shop was only up the road.

"That kind of explains how the animal stuff might've started," I said. "But it doesn't explain all the other stuff in Celeste's garden. The weather, I mean."

Now it was Nan's turn to ponder. "Think about how you felt just before you sneezed or coughed, Fleur? Were you sad, angry, happy, surprised?"

"I felt all of those things at some point but only because of Celeste. Everything was fine before she arrived at school and then everything changed."

"Then I think you already know that's who you need to face. All these tricky emotions are your body's way of letting you know something isn't right. That something or somebody isn't being fair, and if you continue to ignore them–"

The back door opened.

"I've got some, Nell," Mum, said cheerfully. "I'll just get a spoon."

"Let's chat upstairs after tea. I'll think of a way to smuggle you up. Telling the truth doesn't make you weak, it helps to make you stronger. You'll see." Nan wrapped her rose-petal scented arm around my shoulder and squeezed it tight. "Now it's my turn to confess. I've not been entirely honest with you or your mum."

"What is it? Are you poorly again?"

"Certainly not! I'm as fit as a fiddle, plus I feel much better knowing you're okay. I do feel bad for something though."

"It can't be that bad. Tell me; I won't say a word. Not if you don't want me to."

Nan fiddled with the wooden buttons on her cardigan before sheepishly letting out a big sigh. "I finished the last of the horseradish sauce three weeks ago."

# CHAPTER TWENTY-TWO

## *Dad*

In the end, Nan didn't have to smuggle me into her attic-room after tea. She made a thoroughly convincing argument to Mum about how her room provided the most relaxing pre-hockey match environment. She threw in many compliments about how Mum had exquisitely painted the walls, and that she was the sole reason Nan had been able to settle so quickly into a perfectly decorated, beach-like paradise. Wow, she was good!

Sir Barclay left me and Nan to it while he continued to look for Dame Genevieve by following Celeste's movements after school.

We quickly set up a game of chess, an alibi in case Mum came up and found us in the middle of a deep and magical conversation. Nan threw me her little tin of peppermints, which narrowly missed my bishop.

"Feeling better?" she asked, twiddling a mint around in her mouth. I suspected she was trying to get rid of the taste of Mum's jerk chicken and goats' cheese quiche. Especially since she felt obliged to smother it in horseradish sauce after Mum has gone to great lengths to buy some.

I looked at her and smiled. "I am, but I still have loads of questions."

"I'll do my best to answer, fire away!"

I suddenly wished I had made a list.

"When do you think my gifts will work properly? As in, what do I have to do to take control of my emotions?"

"The same thing all Hexters do–we talk and listen, and we follow our instincts and our hearts. Being you is your best asset, Fleur. You don't need anything else. You just haven't realised that yet."

"That's easy to say when you can invisibly fly! My special gifts aren't anywhere near as exciting as yours."

"How do you know? You haven't learnt to control them properly yet. You don't just become magic. You're either born with it or you're not. The only tricky part is that it doesn't always appear straight away. Sometimes it can take years to surface."

"Really? Why?"

"I'm not sure. My grandfather spotted it in me, like I spotted it in you, but mine didn't start to show until I moved away from St. Lucia as a teenager. He said my body was shocked into it. It's a big thing you see, moving to a new country, leaving friends behind, and shifting schools. Big changes in our lives or being away from our normal comforts can really cause havoc with people like you and me."

Nan pointedly peered over the top of her spectacles at me to make sure I had joined up the dots. I suppose the upset of Dad leaving, losing my friends, worrying about Nan, and dealing with Celeste on top of everything else could be seen as big life changes.

"Are you two okay, up there?" Mum shouted up.

"Yes, thanks!" we both replied.

"Doesn't Mum know anything about me? Or you?"

Nan firmly shook her head. "Hexters only discuss magic with other Hexters. It's just easier that way. If the wrong person found out it could be dangerous. I, for one, don't want to be anyone's secret weapon or science experiment, do you?"

The hairs on my arms popped up as I thought about Celeste knowing I was a Hexter and what Mum would do if she ever found out the truth about me being a Hexter too.

"But Mum wouldn't hurt us or tell anyone, would she?" I quivered.

"This is where your father and I have a difference of opinion. You see, he was a bit of a late developer, which is fine and totally natural, but he got frustrated with me constantly watching him and asking him about feelings, gifts, and magic. When nothing appeared by the time he left school, he decided enough was enough. I think I put too much pressure on him, which turned him away from believing he was a Hexter at heart."

"That's sad." I toyed with one of Nan's pawns.

"But then he met your mum. Your beautiful, kind, and wonderful mum, who didn't have a Hexter background, but she made him happy. She made us all happy and still does."

"So, what's the problem then?"

"Not a problem as such, but he decided he didn't want anything to do with magic because he liked the carefree feeling of being with someone–" Nan hesitated, tapping her lips with her finger as if she couldn't bring herself to finish.

"Someone what?" I asked, on the edge of the footstool.

"Normal."

I let the natural silence between us flow.

"I don't mean Hexters aren't normal," Nan continued. "But you understand what I'm trying to say?" I nodded. "I'm just trying to explain how your father felt."

"So, he never told Mum? And now she still doesn't know?"

My hands started to twitch. I knew I hadn't been honest with her about Celeste and my gifts, but this suddenly felt like a horrible betrayal.

"I know it's difficult, baby, but he thought he was doing the right thing. By protecting her and you. He didn't want you growing up under the same constant glare. I tried to persuade him many times to tell your mum, because I know how much she loves him, and I know that wouldn't change just because she found out he was a Hexter."

"Do you think he's scared of losing her?" I pinched my cheek and listened harder.

"I do, but I'm worried he already has. Your mum has been very patient with him, but if he doesn't come home soon, I fear that she'll move on. And who could blame her? She thinks he left because he was heartbroken after your Grandpa Willie died. But that wasn't the only reason. It was also because... because..."

"Because what, Nan?"

"Because it triggered his magical gifts!"

"What?" I gasped, banging my knee against Nan's table. "He's got his gifts? They've finally appeared? What are they?" My hands trembled, because although I was beyond excited to hear my dad was a Hexter like me, it also made me miss him more than ever.

"He's a Disalator," Nan said. "That's what made him panic about your mum finding out because he kept disappearing and reappearing in different places. He struggled to think of excuses and, like you, he didn't know how he'd done it either. After all these years of ruling magic out and losing Grandpa Willie at the same time, I think it was too much for him. All he kept saying before he left was that he felt trapped and needed space to figure things out."

Poor Dad. If he was anything like me, no wonder he felt shocked and afraid, especially on top of losing Grandpa Willie. A tiny bit of mint surfaced from beneath my gums, which I quietly crunched.

"Is he only a Disalator then?" I didn't mean to be rude; I was just trying to find out if he had one gift or two gifts like me and Nan.

"Hexters always have two gifts," she said. "But when your dad left, he did so with only one. Even though it was unusual, it didn't matter to me because I was delighted to find out he had at least one gift like his own father." Nan's face beamed.

"Grandpa Willie was a Disalator too?" I shrieked excitedly. This was unreal! How had I spent ten years in a magical family without noticing a thing? Nan nodded. "So was Dad worried his second gift might not appear then?" I narrowed my eyes, confused, and Nan started shuffling about with hankies up her sleeve.

"Ah, well, he wrote to me not long after he left and just before your grandpa's funeral. He said he had started to hear strange voices when he walked around, only they weren't coming from people." Nan pulled her spectacles off altogether and placed them on her lap. "Does that sound familiar to you?"

I gulped. "He's... an Animalator too, isn't he?" My heart started beating faster.

"I think he is, yes, but I told him not to mention it in a letter again in case it fell into the wrong hands... and he hasn't written since." Nan wiped a small tear from her eye. "He will though, Fleur, as soon as he's ready, it's been a lot for him to take in."

"But surely Dad would need you now more than ever, wouldn't he?"

Nan thought for a moment and checked the pockets of her cardigan. "Think how you've been feeling lately with everything that's been going on. What did you do when your feelings mounted up on top of you?"

I slowly exhaled because I had done the same as Dad. I had pushed everyone away and tried to deal with things alone.

"Don't be hard on yourself, it's fine. Everything will start to get better now you've shared your worries, but I guess your father isn't quite ready to share his yet. Maybe he needs more time. But while I promised him that I wouldn't interfere, and I wouldn't tell you or your mum the truth, I also promised him I would help to look after you if you needed me."

Nan smiled and moved her knight forward to take my queen.

"It's sad that Dad isn't with us but I'm glad you're here, and it's nice to think we both have special gifts together. That our family is magic."

"I'll help you anyway I can, but I won't hide things from you anymore. My magic days are almost over." I reached for her hand and squeezed it. "Fun things never last forever, and things change when you get older. You don't have the same strength, speed, or skills as you did at the beginning. My first dizzy spell only confirmed that my gifts are getting weaker the older I get. They're slowly slipping away, but yours, Fleur, are only just beginning!"

"Oh, Nan! I'm sorry!" I rested my head against her arm. I hadn't thought it was possible for Nan's special gifts to diminish. It seemed so unfair.

"It's fine, baby, I knew it would happen. It's one of the downsides of old age and it's been happening for a while. Why else do you think people have reported seeing arms and legs and slippers flying about all over the place?"

I spluttered but covered my outburst with a believable cough into Nan's hankie, for Mum's sake. I knew Nan could invisibly fly, but it was still a surprise to hear her admit it. To confirm it was her in the newspapers all this time.

"It's because my gifts aren't as strong as they used to be. My invisibility just isn't that invisible anymore but just because I can't fly, doesn't mean I can't help you understand your gifts. You've been blessed with a head full of magic, Fleur, so make the most of it while you've still got it."

That sounded good but being able to talk freely to Nan about my feelings and gifts felt even better.

"I'm proud of you for telling me the truth. It's not easy but it's brave."

"I'm not sure I'll be as brave tomorrow. I still haven't figured out a plan for how I'm going to handle Celeste or find Dame Genevieve."

"From what you've said, I think you need to figure out Celeste first. Think about what she does, how she acts, and what she says. If she really is a Hexter, she'll have a gift and even if it hasn't shown yet, maybe there'll be clues."

We sat in silence for a bit and played another game of chess. It felt like we both needed time to think things through. For once, the funny feeling in my tummy was a happier, more excited one, rather than knots of fear. Although Dad wasn't around at the moment, I was lucky to have Mum and Nan by my side. I didn't know how long it would be until Dad decided to come home, but I did know it wouldn't be long before the feathered member of our family returned to his Birdrobe, because of the familiar reappearance of thick clouds, which I had managed to manically swirl outside.

# CHAPTER TWENTY-THREE

## *The Day of the Match*

A sea of proud parents surrounded the hockey pitch as Mr Augustus trotted up and down the white lines with his megaphone. After one final clipboard check, he was ready to introduce the tournament otherwise known as the deciding match–whoever won today's game would compete for the prestigious Farrow Park Cup against the merciless St. Mary's School.

If I wasn't consumed with worry, I would have attempted a cartwheel at the thought of never having to play hockey with Celeste ever again after today. My immediate plan was to keep my ankles out of Celeste's reach, and get through the game as quickly as possible, so that Sir Barclay and I could then follow Celeste to wherever it was she was going next.

Mum had somehow managed to bag her and Nan a front row seat, which was brilliant as I loved having them there. It was also a tad worrying as Mum tended to be even more embarrassing in public and my nerves couldn't handle one of her 'Bottom' jokes right now.

Nan was under strict instructions to sit tight and avoid

all flying manoeuvres, however tempted she might be to help. The only exception was the flapping of her hankie as a warning signal and that was only if Celeste made any sudden movements away from the school premises. Sir Barclay had circled Celeste's house all night but there was still no sign of Dame Genevieve, or any packed articles resembling a birdcage.

"Good afternoon, everyone!" Mr Augustus boomed. His sparkly mustard headband glistened in the afternoon sun. His wig was combed to perfection. "It's lovely to see you all here to celebrate Class Six's last day at Buxworth Primary School."

Everyone cheered loudly, and for once so did I, because I couldn't wait to get it over with.

"To prolong the celebrations, after today's match I'd like to invite you all back to the classroom for refreshments, and a special Show and Tell, which I've promised the children we can do one last time before they leave."

Mr Augustus was loving the fact his voice was louder than usual as he droned on about how much we have all 'matured as a class'.

"So, without further ado, let's get our girls' final intra-school tournament started!" The crowd launched into applause as my mouth dried up. "3. . . 2. . . 1."

He blew the whistle, and we were off! I could see Mum's face in the front row, her arms already performing a solo Mexican wave in excitement at watching me run. It was a shame she hadn't realised that I was frantically trying to run away from Celeste who was hot on the trail of my ankles.

I had put Nan's hand-carved chess piece, the castle with ivy growing up the side, into my shorts pocket first thing this morning. I wanted it with me for luck–not that it appeared to be working. It was also my chosen object for Mr Augustus's Show and Tell assignment after the match, assuming I could still walk by then.

Celeste wasn't in the least bit bothered that she was being watched by every parent from our class, mainly because her own parents were nowhere in sight, which explained her stinkier than usual mood as she thundered up the pitch with a face that was longer than her hockey stick.

*WHACK!*

Suki was down—she had been hooked by Celeste who charged towards Ruby at tremendous speed. A bit of fancy footwork between the two players ensued, followed by a Celeste hip-shove towards Tiggy, which immediately stopped her from swiping the ball away. The yellows were alight.

"GOAL!" Mr Augustus shouted.

How was it 1-0 to the yellows already? We didn't have a hope of winning. The reds quickly gathered for a pre-whistle word of encouragement.

"They can't beat us today!" Leena growled. "Not after yesterday's practice match. We've worked just as hard as they have. The only difference being, we haven't used dirty tactics!"

There was more than a whiff of defeat in the air after the yellows' early goal. It hung over us like steel armour.

"Let's try our best and keep going," I said. "It'll soon be over."

"You're doing really well, girls," Mr Augustus encouraged. "Stay focused!"

It was hard to stay focused when you had a random butterfly attached to your shoulder, its flimsy legs stuck to my T-shirt and not letting go. Not even as leaves rustled violently above my head. Without warning, out poked a familiar face from a wobbly branch.

"*Squawk!* Get a shift on, Fleur. You won't win the game standing still and we need to find Dame Genevieve! You've got to confront Celeste the minute you get a chance."

Was I glad to see old fluff-pants! We didn't get a chance to properly speak last night or this morning.

"I'll try," I said through my teeth, pretending to smile so that nobody noticed me talking to Sir Barclay. "But Celeste looks pretty powerful and devious today."

"*Squawk!* Nonsense, you're taking the easy way out!"

"I am not!" I said defiantly.

I could run as fast as the next person, but whenever Celeste ran towards me, I looked for a way to best protect my ankles rather than helping to set up a goal. A fine team player I was turning out to be.

Sir Barclay stayed tucked away on his branch as the crowd fixed on Celeste. The butterfly, which appeared to be a Red Admiral, remained glued to my shoulder. It flashed its pretty hues of black and red, which were far more delicate than what suddenly came out of its mouth.

"Will you two stop arguing!" it murmured. "Unless of course you want to be flattened like a pancake."

"*Squawk!* She's right, Fleur, they're coming towards us! Get the ball off Ruby and pass it to Rudi on your right. Do it now, quickly! You can do this!"

It was hard wrestling with Ruby because she was in a defiant mood too and kept hogging the ball, but after a few taps and turns, I did it! Sir Barclay's plan had worked. I dribbled the ball down the pitch away from the opposition. Perhaps there were some perks to being the only one able to hear animals all over the place. I slid the ball across to Rudi who zipped it towards Lydia, who passed it to Jasmine.

*GOAL!*

It was 1-1. I couldn't believe it! Nothing like that had ever happened to me before.

"*Squawk!* Now, that's what I'm talking about, Fleur! Well done!"

Mum frantically waved and gave me the thumbs-up, which, although was a bit embarrassing given I hadn't scored the actual goal, felt fantastic. For the first time since we started practising this frightful sport, I was actually enjoying it.

No rest for the wicked–we were off again! This time I chased Anais, who had been slipped the ball by Celeste and was now heading towards Ruby to make another sly pass.

"*Squawk!* Get in front of her, Fleur! Quickly!"

"Yeah, what he said!" chirruped a blackbird who was sat amongst a long row of others all clinging to any available space in the old oak tree. "This is the best match we've seen in years!"

I ran as fast as I could. The ball was in sight–it was mine!

"*Squawk!* Tap it to Rudi now," Sir Barclay said. "That's it, now turn it to Beau, who with any luck will ping it to Lydia in front of her. *Squawk!* That's it, Fleur."

Sir Barclay and I were proving to be a winning combination as he surreptitiously flew from tree to tree thinking up the best strategies to beat the yellows.

Celeste spluttered louder than our rusty old car. "No!" she ranted at her teammates. "Don't give the game away! Hurry up, you useless twits!"

*GOAL!*

It was too late. We were another point up. The reds were officially beating the pants off the yellows.

"Nice work, Fleur!" Leena shouted. "Maybe we can do this after all!"

*WHACK!*

Our glory moment was short-lived as Celeste pelted the ball across to Anais, who somehow managed to equalise our triumphant goal within seconds. It was 2-2. There was absolutely no way I was going to let Celeste wipe the floor with us again.

I sprinted to wrestle the ball from Celeste's clutches, but the sweat on my palms loosened the grip on my hockey stick, which suddenly met with something heavy.

"You did that on purpose, you imbecile!" Celeste shrieked. She was slumped over her own stick on the floor, her sweaty skin red and shiny.

"Sorry, I didn't mean to," I said, offering my hand to help her up.

She immediately pushed it away and crawled onto her knees.

"Is everything alright, girls?" Mr Augustus called from the far side.

Celeste had her back to him, fiercely pulling up her socks.

I gave him a hesitant thumbs-up and shouted, "We're fine. Play on, we'll only be a minute."

Mr Augustus blew a short whistle to continue the game, while Celeste fiddled with her socks.

"Oh, what does it matter anyway!" she barked. "I'm flying

out of this dump to New York at midnight so what's the point? Consider yourself promoted to the winning team, Fleur, because it's not like my lot are capable of victory without me! Look at them!"

I did. They were at the far end of the pitch battling it out against Leena, Lydia, Azari, and Beau, who were dominating the ball beautifully. The reds might not be the fastest, or the fiercest, but they were playing as a team and listening to each other brilliantly, which was more than the yellows had ever done. All they were capable of doing was listening to Celeste's angry shouts and doing as they were told.

"I think they're trying their best," I said, clenching my hockey stick, firmly this time.

"Shame the same can't be said for you." Celeste bounced up from the ground and aggressively wiped the mud off her shorts. "Alright, then, feather-face. Let's do this! Let's see how special you really are."

We raced towards the others, side-by-side, but then Celeste ran a few strides ahead, a deafening silence bubbling between us until she couldn't help herself any longer.

"Is that as fast as you can go, Fleur? All that fighting talk back there, it almost sounded like you had it in you and yet here we are!" She smirked. "Watch out, Fleur, Elsie Steaddington and her invincible Springalator gifts are poised to replace you when you're ready to admit defeat. That old bat's got more spring in her knees than you ever will!"

What the? How could Celeste possibly know that our super-slow, Zimmer-frame-wheeling neighbour, Elsie Steaddington was a Springalator? Or what a Springalator even was? Nan had only written down Elsie's name in her book and the rest was blank. She hadn't figured out what her special gift was, only that she suspected she had one.

I pushed my legs harder until I was neck and neck with Celeste. She pinched the ball from Anais, and selfishly hogged it until she had managed to steer it away from the reds, but she hadn't steered it away from me. I pulled the ball away from her.

"How would you know anything about Elsie Steaddington or Springalators?" I panted, not letting her anywhere near the ball.

"Forget it!" Celeste said. "I just meant that. . . that you're slow!"

She hadn't just meant that, and I wasn't going to give her the ball or let her wriggle out of an explanation. Something didn't add up. How did she know about Elsie's knees? There was nobody watching apart from me the other day when she somersaulted over her fence. I had seen it through Nan's supersonic telescope and checked everywhere to see if anyone else was around. If Celeste was hiding in the park behind a tree I would have seen her. I was determined to get to the bottom of it and do exactly as Nan had said last night–follow my instincts.

"No, you didn't. That's not what you meant. You mentioned Elsie's knees and how would you know anything about that?"

Celeste didn't respond. Instead, she tried to elbow me out of the way and desperately reclaim the ball.

"Oh no you don't!" I yelled as I managed to tap the ball to Leena who had appeared on my left-hand side.

*WHACK!*

Leena knocked the ball miles away from us, belting it back down to Beau who was waiting patiently in the wings.

"Aaagh! You stupid, annoying birdbrain!" Celeste screamed. Her face dropped altogether when she saw Beau smash the ball to Tiggy. "You might think you're smart, Fleur, but you're not. Your nan wrote all about Elsie Steaddington's amazing somersaults in that book of hers. What's the matter? Can't you read properly now either?"

Celeste chased the action as my head began to spin. I wasn't stupid, I knew exactly what Elsie had done because I had seen it with my own eyes through a telescope. I hadn't seen it written in Nan's book!

The crowd was focused purely on the reds who were fending off the yellows' attempts to regain control of the ball. Beau was having none of it and skilfully knocked it between two yellow players' bandy legs before catching it again the other side.

*GOAL!*

The reds and the parents went berserk! They jumped up and down on the grass as we scooped the lead, 3-2 against the yellows. I didn't know what came over me but the next thing I heard was a. . .

*THUMP!*

Celeste had faceplanted the mud because I had hooked her ankle.

"I'm not stupid!" I said. "My nan hadn't written anything down about Elsie Steaddington in her book because she was in hospital." Celeste rolled onto her back to face me. "And even if she wasn't, it still wouldn't have been in her book because I'd already lost it!"

A eureka moment lit my brain like a fluorescent light. Celeste was a gift-spotter like Nan, a Spyalator, which meant she could sense magic in others. Pieces of the jigsaw clicked together in my head as Celeste's bulgy eyes locked with mine.

# CHAPTER TWENTY-FOUR

## *Spyalator*

Mr Augustus halted the game and dashed over to us, his whistle bouncing from shoulder to shoulder. The yellows huddled together to discuss much-needed tactics, while the reds hugged and grabbed each other by the neck in raw excitement.

"Everything alright, you two? What's the matter now?"

Celeste hopped up into a burpee and rubbed her cheeks to check for any traces of mud. "No, everything's not alright!" she said.

By now, both teams had noticed the on-pitch entertainment. The parents also looked on curiously before taking the opportunity to talk amongst themselves in the baking sun.

"Fleur tripped me up on purpose!" she howled.

"Fleur is this true?" he asked, surprised.

"I'm sorry, Mr Augustus," I said shuffling my hand over Nan's chess piece which was still hanging on to the lining of my shorts pocket. "I didn't mean... my hand... just... sort of felt a bit funny... almost numb-ish!"

Her lips were so crunched up inside her mouth that it made her look as if she didn't have any lips at all.

Who was I? I had tripped Celeste up, used the same excuse she gave to Mr Augustus when she tripped Leena up, and discovered she too had a special gift.

"Be a bit more careful, please," Mr Augustus said. "I know it's tough in this heat, but you're all playing really well. Grab yourselves a quick drink, and let's go back for the finale in five, okay?"

I nodded. Celeste folded her arms, which was as much agreement as Mr Augustus was going to get. Mr Augustus walked off and here was my chance.

"You're a Spyalator, aren't you?" I whispered, as the others hurried to their water bottles away from us. "You can sense people with magic gifts. That's why you're always watching me and looking at me funny."

It was all fitting together. Why else would she have been so mean to me since she arrived?

"Well, you're not exactly brilliant at hiding your gifts, are you?" Celeste smoothed down her fringe and sighed. "It's alright for you, both your gifts have appeared and they're both exciting. You can actually do something with them, but I've only got one gift and what can I do with that? Nothing! I mean, what's even the point in having a gift if you can't do anything with it? Apart from watch morons like you struggle to cope."

She had a nerve! I wasn't that bad!

"I'm fed up with watching! Always a spectator and never a competitor. You should try it sometime and see how you like it."

I wondered if this was why she was such a brute on the hockey pitch. Because it was one of the few places where she was in charge of her own destiny.

"Celeste! What's going on? Are you okay?" Ruby and Anais ventured over to us, but Celeste quickly shot them down.

"Leave me alone for a minute, I'm thinking about my technique. I'll come over in a sec."

They looked stunned that Celeste had binned them off to talk to me. Tutting loudly, they flounced off, unimpressed at being shunned.

"Don't you have another gift as well as being a gift-spotter?" I bravely asked, knowing full well that Hexters always have two gifts.

"You mean, can I also fly about all over town dropping green and purple slippers everywhere like your nan?"

My stomach tensed.

"No, I can't do anything else. Much to the annoyance of my parents, but like they keep saying, I'm sure it will appear when I least expect it." Celeste blew up towards her fringe.

Leena, Lydia and Beau kept looking at me and their watches. We didn't have long left.

"Oh, right, yes I'm sure it will." The silence between us was awkward. "What happened to your parrot?" I said, changing the subject and trying to sound nonchalant even though every toe was crossed inside my trainers for useful information.

"I've no idea," she replied. "It's gone. After you turned up in our back garden, and Mum found out I'd been secretly keeping it in our shed, she got rid of it. I haven't seen it since."

My heart sank. We had lost Dame Genevieve for good. The laurel hedge in the distance shook left and right. I could tell it was Sir Barclay's signature flap. Poor Sir Barclay. I was dreading giving him the update.

"That's him again, isn't it?" Celeste asked, looking up at

the tree. "Your nan's parrot from the other night? I can hear him squawking but that's it. What is he doing here?"

She twizzled her hockey stick around in her hand sullenly. It must've been hard for her not having any actual magic of her own, although I was sure being a gift-spotter must have some uses.

"Oh, he wanted to watch us play," I said dryly.

I didn't see the need to mention he was stalking her every move, trying to find his wife.

"*Squawk!* Get ready, Fleur! He's on his way!"

Mr Augustus blew his whistle and Celeste whizzed off for the ball as predicted.

"Give us a shout if you need us, Fleur, and we'll help too." One of the thick-set crows from yesterday made an appearance in the trees which were brimming with wildlife.

It was incredibly kind of Sir Barclay to offer his birds eye hockey hints, but I wanted to beat Celeste fair and square. Nan was watching us from her chair, putting a questioning thumb up and down as if to ask if we were okay. I gave her a thumbs-up.

"Sir Barclay, please don't take this the wrong way or anything, but would you mind if I did this on my own? It's not that I'm not grateful."

"*Squawk!* Of course, I don't mind, Fleur. Just please get a shift on because I think we should expand our search for Dame Genevieve afterwards. *Squawk!*"

"Hurry up, Fleur!" Mr Augustus said.

I raced off after the ball. I wasn't wobbly or nervous or sad, I was on fire because my mood had brought about even brighter and hotter sunshine.

Celeste's shrieks were as loud as ever, but so far everyone on the red team was vertical, which meant that she hadn't knocked anyone down yet.

"Up front, Ruby!" Celeste yelled.

Ruby did as she was told and knocked the ball on to Anais, who didn't realise Lydia was so close to her. I could see Leena up ahead and Emi on my right. Suki's stick went in for the ball and she got it!

"Pass it here, Suki!"

"Gladly!" Suki knocked the ball across to me.

"Over here, Fleur!"

I passed the ball over to Emi in the nick of time. Celeste dived for it simultaneously but missed the ball by inches. We both headed up in tandem to follow Emi.

"Mark her, Anais! Mark her!" Celeste barked, but Anais wasn't fast enough.

Emi slipped the ball to Leena. I ran as fast as I could to catch up with Leena, and Celeste made a run for it too. We were neck and neck until I purposefully withdrew and moved to the side. Leena's ankles took a pasting from Celeste, but she managed to twist and turn.

*TAP!*

Leena fired the ball across to me as I found myself impressively ahead of the others, and in the perfect place at the perfect time.

"Do it, Fleur!" Leena shouted.

I did and I scored!

Mr Augustus blew his whistle three times, and the game was finished. The crowd cheered and clapped, overjoyed. We had won!

"*Squawk!* Well done, Fleur! You did it and all on your own*! Squawk!*"

I looked around as trees and bushes exploded with birds, squirrels, and other creatures, who then stampeded the pitch to cheer for me. Nan was on her feet next to Mum, who kept waving even when everybody else gradually stopped. The yellows were motionless apart from the odd placing of their heads in their hands in despair. Celeste ignored them all, choosing to shake her head in disgust, and pack up her water bottle and jumper as fast as she could.

"You did it, Fleur!"

Suddenly, I was being hugged by my teammates. It felt incredible and much nicer than having sore or painful ankles.

"We did it together!" I replied. Over Leena's shoulder I could see Celeste walking across the field. "One second, guys."

I pulled away and ran until I was by Celeste.

"No congratulations?" I teased.

"Beginners' luck!" she replied, but she was smiling. An actual friendly smile.

"At your next school, if you spot anyone with a magical gift, maybe you could strike up a pleasant conversation for a change? You might not love being Spyalator, or a Hexter, but it might be cool to be a good friend."

"Yeah maybe," Celeste said, smoothing her fringe.

"I hope your parrot turns up before you leave," I said, to doubly, triply, ensure she didn't know where Dame Genevieve was.

"I doubt it." She shrugged. "Mum wouldn't have hurt it, but I don't expect I'll see it again. Her and Dad are

Springalators and Magnalators, you see." Celeste paused to gauge my reaction.

I tried hard not to move my eyebrows, but they automatically zipped further up my fascinated forehead; my sudden intake of breath was a dead giveaway too.

"But they're only interested in two things," she continued. "Their own magic, and whether my second gift has appeared. It's exhausting! I don't suppose I've got time for a parrot anyway. Not if there are as many after-school activities as Mum says there are in America, and that's without the shopping malls, swimming parks, and cheerleading classes."

She was doing her best to make it sound fun and exciting, but I wasn't convinced. Ruby and Anais shouted over for her before we reached the classroom.

"Well, I hope it all works out for you."

"Hope you figure out how to control what you've got too, and if I ever see you again, I hope I won't need sunhats, gloves, wellies, and umbrellas!"

I laughed. "So do I! Look, you're already a true Hexter you know, even if your second gift hasn't appeared yet. Maybe if you used your Spyalator gift in a more positive way, it could help? It's got to be worth a shot, right?"

"Maybe. . . it doesn't sound as much fun, but you could have a point." She looked down at the ground before staring back at me. "Listen, I still think libraries are boring, and I don't get the obsession with chess but, I was wrong about you, Fleur, and I'm sorry. You're not so bad after all."

I snorted. "Thanks. . . I think."

It wasn't the most gushing apology ever, but at least she had had the guts to say it to my face.

"I suppose, I was a bit jealous of you and the fact you've got two gifts. You don't have to constantly try to impress or overcompensate for something you don't have. You're naturally gifted on your own and if anyone suggests otherwise then–"

"Then what? Tell someone, as long as it isn't Mr Augustus?!"

We both smiled. I wasn't trying to make her feel bad or slate our teacher, but she had said enough, and I was ready to move on from the drama of everything.

"No, well, yes, sort of. What I'd actually do is ignore them because they probably don't fully know what they're on about anyway."

I nodded and so did she. A warm feeling floated throughout my body because I knew that things were going to be very different after today. For both of us.

# CHAPTER TWENTY-FIVE

## *Show and Tell*

It was stifling in the classroom after our match. Not only because we had worked up a glow on the pitch, but because our parents had squeezed into the back of the classroom for our last ever Show and Tell.

This Show and Tell was special because Mr Augustus had asked us to each bring in an item that reminded us of our time at primary school. The only catch was, we had to explain why it was special to us. It was a bit like having a giant memory box made up from the whole class.

Although my mind had been on other things this last term, I had chosen my Show and Tell item weeks ago.

"Thank you, Lydia, now it's your turn, Celeste." Mr Augustus nodded to the space in front of the SMART Board where she proudly displayed her hockey stick.

I was convinced it held lots of girls' blood DNA within its fibres due to the years of ankle whacking.

"This is my favourite hockey stick and it's special to me because it's got a sticker from every school I've ever attended."

I had always been too busy running away from Celeste to

notice the little stickers that were proudly lined up along the bottom of her hockey stick. There were at least fifteen of them scattered along the wood, each representing a different school that she had attended over the years. It was incredible to think that she had moved around the world so much and at such a young age, it must have been tough at times settling in to a new place and a new school, trying to make new friends, but that didn't seem to matter to her right now, as she proudly paraded her stick in front of everyone in the room, delighted to be talking about the sport she loved the most.

"Thank you, Celeste," Mr Augustus said. "And here's a little memento to remind you of your time here at Buxworth Primary when you leave for your big American dream tonight."

Ruby wiped the corners of her puffy eyes when Mr Augustus mentioned Celeste leaving. She had burst into tears earlier when I overheard Celeste telling her and Anais that she was leaving, and I wondered how they would both function without her. Celeste blushed as Mr Augustus pressed a smart gold sticker firmly onto her hockey stick next to the others.

"And last but not least, Fleur! It's over to you."

I walked to the front of the class and reached into my pocket, finally able to pull out the offending item, which had dug into my thigh all through the match. I glanced at Mum and Nan who stared back in return with glazed eyes. Nan had already reached for her hanky to wipe a small tear from her eye.

Nan's chess piece was a work of art. Every leaf hand-carved within the soft wood, and its enchanting castle doors that had led to endless games and hours of fun. This was precisely the reason I had chosen it.

"This is a chess piece from my home set where I play with my nan all the time. She's much better at chess than I am, even though she is eighty-nine, but I love playing it with her. I've loved every minute of playing chess here at school too, but I haven't played much recently." I saw Ruby and Anais shuffle sheepishly on the carpet. "I've made brilliant memories over the years and I'm really looking forward to making some new ones, maybe with some of you again too if we're in the same class at Shepson High after the holidays. If I've learnt anything though, it's to enjoy all games. Even the ones you think you dislike, because you never know, they might lead you on an exciting adventure that you didn't know was possible."

Leena, Beau, and the rest of the reds were the first to cheer.

"Bravo!" Mr Augustus clapped alongside all the parents. "That was brilliant, Fleur. What a wonderful way to finish the celebration of all our lovely school memories. Right, children, if your grownup is here, you may leave!"

It was like a gun had been fired, as children and parents alike leapt up from their chairs, gathered their belongings, and raced to the door as fast as they could. Mum waited patiently near the craft-drawers, a hand gently supporting Nan's elbow. She threw her arms around me and planted a huge smacker on my cheek.

"Well done, Fleur! You were fantastic! I'm so proud of you," Mum said.

Nan squeezed my hand as I made my way to my locker. "That's my girl!" she whispered gently.

I was happy. Not because it was the last day of primary school or because I had survived the hockey tournament, but because I felt stronger and free.

"Right then, as a special treat for a special win, how about we have something special for tea. Something like. . . "

I cringed at the thought of what Mum was about to suggest. My tastebuds weren't up to her three-bean bouyon, jerk chicken and goats' cheese quiche, or anything else engineered by her fair hands for that matter.

"Takeaway pizza!" she announced.

"At last, something decent!" Nan blurted as Mum's mouth dropped open. "Sorry, what I meant was that sounds like an excellent idea!"

"Yes please!" I said.

Celeste tried to look busy in the corridor as she waited for her mum to pick her up. A lorry containing a load of brand-new hockey sticks wouldn't have altered the look on her face.

"See you later then, Celeste," I said softly, as Nan shot around and gave Celeste a parting glare. Mum held her by the elbow and guided her out ahead of me. "Hope your flight goes okay."

"I'm sure it will," she replied. "The forecast isn't suggesting anything unusual, so we should be perfectly fine."

Even if Celeste had stayed around here, I doubted she would *ever* let me forget my fear-generated thunderstorm in her garden.

I waved at her as I followed Mum and Nan to the exit. Ruby and Anais approached me as I stepped outside and into the warm air.

"Fleur wait up!" Anais called, with Ruby beside her.

I glanced at Nan, who nodded at me. I didn't have anything to say to them, but I was going to be the bigger person.

"Well done for the match. You played really well."

"Thanks," I said. "It was a close one, but we got there in the end." I tapped the clasp of my bag because I didn't really know what else to say. Thanks for joining forces with Celeste and making this term a misery?

Ruby sidled closer too. "We're hanging out at the park on Saturday afternoon, if you fancy joining us. It'll be like old times."

I had spent weeks pining for the three of us to play together like we always had. Giggling, drawing, playing chess, but the thought of catching up with them had suddenly lost its appeal. Hexters and non-Hexters all make mistakes, but life was too short to waste it on mean people.

"Fleur!" Leena shouted from the doorway, drawing my attention. "See you Saturday afternoon?"

"Definitely!" I said. "See you later!"

I turned back to Ruby and Anais who both frowned.

"Sorry, girls, I can't make this Saturday," I said breezily. "I'm out with some friends!"

My feet were fizzing, although strangely not from all the running. I couldn't quite describe it. Definitely not an ache, but possibly a throb, it was more of a prickly tickle than a twinge of pain. So the arrival of three delicious pizzas from Mission Impizzable were a welcome distraction.

"*Squawk!* Is now really the time for pizza? I thought we

were going to follow Celeste as soon as we dropped your mum and nan off?" Sir Barclay had flown down from Nan's attic-room and perched his feathery bottom on the banister nodule in the hallway. He watched me approach.

I nervously scrunched the neck of my T-shirt and felt a sudden pang of guilt. In the excitement of winning the match and leaving school on okay terms with everyone, I hadn't thought about how I would break the news to Sir Barclay that Celeste's mum had shifted Dame Genevieve somewhere, and even Celeste didn't know where she was.

"Here you are, Sir Barclay." I handed him a substantial piece of cheesy stuffed crust. "Listen, about that, I've got something I need to tell you."

"*Squawk*! I'm listening," he said between beakfuls.

"Hurry up, Fleur! Come through, it's time for a toast," Mum shouted.

I peered in the dining room and then back at Sir Barclay who had almost finished his stuffed crust.

"Give me two minutes and then I'll explain."

I returned to the table and quickly filled our cups with orange juice.

"Here's to the summer holidays and new beginnings at Shepson High!" Mum said, raising her favourite hot air balloon mug.

"Here, here!" Nan said. "What would you like to do tomorrow, Fleur? It's your first Saturday as a free agent with me in charge while your mum's at work."

"Actually, I've got the day off."

Mum didn't seem hugely ecstatic about her extra day off and I wondered why, but Nan beat me to it.

"Did Mr Bowland sack you?" Nan asked.

"Certainly not!" Mum replied. "Let's just say, I agreed to take something off his hands, which was fast becoming a nuisance." She sounded more guarded than usual.

"Thick gloves?" Nan chortled.

Mum shook her head in exasperation then stomped into the kitchen where she opened the back door and shut it again. She returned clutching a strange-shaped container covered with a purple, crushed velvet cloth.

"No, this thing!" She plonked it on the table on top of last night's *Evening Gazette*. Although the headline was now obscured, I could still make out **Case Dropped Due to Inconclusive Slipper Evidence.**

"That's a birdcage!" I mumbled from the opposite side of the table with a mouthful of pizza.

"Indeed, it is, smarty-pants! Mr Bowland insisted I try to rehome it, as it's too noisy in the antique shop–he's had a headache for days! Some snooty woman brought it in to us earlier in the week and refused to leave without us taking it from her. Something about moving to America and the cage being valuable."

I quickly swallowed my pizza.

"Is it empty?" I asked leaning forwards animatedly.

My eyes narrowed and so did Nan's as Mum lifted the purple cloth.

# CHAPTER TWENTY-SIX

## *Another Exciting New Day*

There was another African Grey parrot but this one had spotty tail feathers!

"Dame Genevieve!" I shouted as Sir Barclay flapped his wings in the hallway.

Dame Genevieve appeared utterly flummoxed inside the scratched, gold-painted cage. I bet she hadn't expected to see us in a million years!

"Who?" Mum frowned.

"Oh, err, we've been learning about kings and queens in history lately," I lied. "They had some really funny names! Don't you think she looks like a Dame Genevieve?"

"*Squawk*!" Sir Barclay's distant flapping became more ferocious as he made his way along the hallway and into the dining room. He brushed his wings repeatedly against the heavy door, his squawks now louder and more frenzied. He squeezed his head through the dining room door and swooped towards the table where he landed on top of the cage, squawking and clawing in desperation to get inside.

"Sir Barclay! You're here!" Dame Genevieve said.

"Where did he come from?" Mum said, alarmed. "Fleur, did you let him out? Shoo! Sir Barclay! Shoo!"

"Open the cage, Mum!" I shouted above the manic flapping from the pair of reunited parrots, whose feathers were creating a vortex of wind around us. "Quick! Hurry up and open the door before they hurt themselves."

"Or peck my pizza!" Nan added unhelpfully.

"*Squawk!* Get her out, Fleur!" Sir Barclay pleaded.

"Calm down, Dame Genevieve," I whispered. "You're safe now. We'll have you out in a jiffy."

Dame Genevieve tempered her wings and moved further back in the cage.

"We'll look after you, I promise."

"Thank you, Fleur! I know you will," Dame Genevieve replied, clicking her beak.

I opened the metal latch. Dame Genevieve flew straight into the wings of Sir Barclay, and they both flapped around each other mid-air, ecstatic at being reunited.

"Well, I never!" Nan said. "What are the chances of finding Sir Barclay the perfect companion?"

She winked at me.

"I said I'd try to rehome it," Mum said. "Not that we're keeping another one! They'll make too much mess, and I can't cope with another fussy pineapple cheese and cracker eater."

Was she serious? We couldn't split them up again. They belonged together!

"How about you let her stay if I help Nan look after them both?" I asked. "It's no trouble, and I'll even do the shopping for them too if that helps?"

Sir Barclay and I were now a team. Who would have thought it possible?

Mum frowned. "But you can't stand Sir Barclay! Why the sudden change of heart?"

He was beyond doubt the most infuriating parrot I had ever met. His ego was enormous, and the air of superiority he wafted around was akin to royalty, but we had come through for one another in the end.

"Well, he's part of the family, isn't he? We've got to look after each other or we don't work properly, do we?"

Mum put the purple cloth on the back of the chair and scooped me into a hug.

"I was determined not to cry again today!" she said, sniffing. "I still can't believe my baby is ready for high school, but with words like that, I know you're more than ready. I love you my littlest Bottom!"

We both giggled as she kissed me on the cheek.

Nan settled back in her place at the table and winked at me as my eye caught hers before she finally finished the last slice of pizza.

It had been an extraordinary day. I waited until Sir Barclay and Dame Genevieve flew upstairs, then followed them both up to Nan's attic-room to see how they were settling in together. They were nestled in the corner of Sir Barclay's Birdrobe, their tailfeathers wrapped snugly around each other as though they had never been apart.

"What a day, Sir Barclay! Can you believe it? We actually

found her," I said, as Sir Barclay turned around, looking content, his feathers neatly groomed and his beak shining bright. "Well, I suppose technically Mum did, but it's amazing, isn't it?

"*Squawk!* Yes, it is, Fleur, and so are you." Dame Genevieve kept her eyes shut, seemingly exhausted from the day's events. "You should be very proud of yourself. It took real grit and maturity to do what you did on that pitch today, to face your fears and stand up to Celeste, and without magic too! *Squawk!*"

"If I'm going to win at something, I want to win it in my own right, without cheating or using any of my magical gifts. Plus, I've got you lot, haven't I? Which is more than Celeste has, so the way I see it, we've all come out as winners, haven't we?"

Sir Barclay pecked Dame Genevieve's sleepy cheek before nodding at me in agreement.

"Can I get you anything, Dame Genevieve?" I asked. "Cheese, biscuits, nuts?"

"No thank you, Fleur. You've done more than enough for me and more than enough for both of us."

Sir Barclay ushered me away from Dame Genevieve and flapped over to the wardrobe at the end of the wall, the one with a couple of Nan's coats in, which he opened with his beak.

"*Squawk!* I've got something for you inside your nan's red suitcase."

He flew back to Dame Genevieve, leaving me to heave out the old suitcase and plonk it in the middle of the floor.

"What's inside?" I lifted the suitcase lid to reveal row upon row of empty cracker packets.

"*Squawk!* Honestly, Fleur, just open them up and stop asking questions for once, will you?"

Inside each cracker packet, there was at least one chess piece from at least two of our sets.

"Sir Barclay! You scoundrel! I knew it was you."

I had lost count of how many had disappeared mid-game when I was at school. I thought it was only a handful he had pinched but there were loads!

"Crikey, Sir Barclay! How many are there?"

"*Squawk!* Fourteen at the last count, but there's something else for you, an early birthday present, in the suitcase pocket. I nipped onto your mum's laptop and ordered one the other night, so please say it was you if she asks."

I unzipped the side-pocket and found a brand-new animal chess set, still in its cellophane wrapper. It was fantastic!

"*Squawk!* It's for you, Fleur," he said apologetically. "And your nan. It would appear you might have a spot of catching up to do."

I was so happy that I wanted to squawk!

"Tell you what," I said, tidying up the cracker packets. "How about I teach you how to play this weekend? Then I can beat your feathered tush legitimately without launching any of Nan's feather cushions at you!"

"*Squawk!* You're on!" he replied.

Nan appeared in the doorway of her room with Mum close behind.

"Come on, Fleur," Mum said, frowning. "It's been a busy day. Let's leave your nan to get some rest."

"But we haven't even had one game yet!"

"I know, I'm only kidding. You two can play as long as

you like tonight but you know where I am if you want to join me for *Tat and That.*"

Yes! I knew she was a legend really. Mum playfully nipped my nose with her fingers then headed downstairs.

I lay in bed that night thinking about all the things that had happened to me over the weeks, and how lucky I was to have Mum, Nan, and not one, but two pompous feather-bums. It was strange to think of Celeste up in the air on her way to America for another new adventure, but I was excited to think about the new adventures I might have as a Hexter.

Mum clambered up the stairs to my bedroom.

"Goodnight, my hockey superstar!" she whispered, kissing my forehead.

I held her hand and squeezed it tight. Once Mum had shut my bedroom door, I closed my eyes and smiled. There were still so many unanswered questions about my magical gifts, but hopefully things would become clearer the more I practiced. You would think being dishonest to Mum would come easily, wouldn't you? Given how much I had fibbed about her dodgy cooking and Celeste's bullying.

It wasn't easy, and I didn't like it one bit, but I trusted Nan's judgement, and I really hoped that Dad would come home soon so that we could all work things out together. Thank goodness I had Nan–I knew she would always listen and try her best to help me understand. Whatever happened next, I knew that she would be there for me when I needed her most–no matter what.

I snuggled under the covers and realised, for the first time in ages, that I was peaceful, happy, and comfortable. Comfortable as a Hexter, as an Animalator, as a Meteolator, and as Fleur Marie Bottom. Mum was right. A comfortable Bottom is a happy Bottom.

# ABOUT THE AUTHOR

Sarah lives in Yorkshire and worked as a Criminologist until she fell in love with writing and quickly swapped a life with crime for a life with rhyme! She is married with three awesome kids who keep her on her toes whilst she is plotting and sharing her latest stories.

Sarah has self-published two picture books. The King and the Cockerel was a finalist in the Wishing Shelf Book Awards in 2018 and Molly's Magic Brolly picked up a Silver Award in 2019. She is currently working on a number of middle grade and children's picture books and has a couple of book club novels up her sleeve too. When she is not writing, she loves nothing more than to run, bike or swim in the hills of Holmfirth and recently entered her first Triathlon. Next New Year's Eve, she will not be making any sports related resolutions.

Sarah is an active SCBWI Member and a Volunteer Ambassador for Candlelighters Charity.

Follow Sarah @SMorrellAuthor
www.sarahmorrellauthor.co.uk